PUFFIN

WHO'S A

AND OTHER STR

Who's afraid? Well, of course, everybody is – of *something*. These gripping stories explore the possibilities – hair-raising, spine-chilling, blood-curdling.

Here's something for everyone who enjoys a good scare. Ghosts range from an evil kitchen-boy with a recipe for death to a tiresome invalid at the top of an apple tree. There's Old Nick himself in one story, and a tale of second-sight, and even a ghost story especially for dog-lovers.

Since the publication of her classic books *Tom's Midnight Garden* and *A Dog So Small*, Philippa Pearce has established a reputation as one of the outstanding writers for children today. *Who's Afraid? and Other Strange Stories* is a winning team of eleven stories and is an enjoyably spooky successor to her earlier book *The Shadow-Cage and Other Tales of the Supernatural*.

Philippa Pearce was born and brought up in the Cambridgeshire village where she now lives. Between then and now were twenty-five years, spent mostly in London. There she worked as a scriptwriter and producer in radio, for the school broadcasting service of the BBC, then as the children's editor of André Deutsch Ltd.

Other books by Philippa Pearce

PHILIPPA PEARCE

and
Other Strange Stories

Illustrated by Peter Melnyczuk

PUFFIN BOOKS

PUFFIN BOOKS

Published by the Penguin Group
Penguin Books Ltd, 27 Wrights Lane, London W8 5TZ, England
Viking Penguin, a division of Penguin Books USA Inc.
375 Hudson Street, New York, New York 10014, USA
Penguin Books Australia Ltd, Ringwood, Victoria, Australia
Penguin Books Canada Ltd, 2801 John Street, Markham, Ontario, Canada L3R 1B4
Penguin Books (NZ) Ltd, 182–190 Wairau Road, Auckland 10, New Zealand

Penguin Books Ltd, Registered Offices: Harmondsworth, Middlesex, England

This collection first published by Viking Kestrel 1986
Published in Puffin Books 1988
3 5 7 9 10 8 6 4

Printed in England by Clays Ltd, St Ives plc
Filmset in Sabon

Contents

A Christmas Pudding Improves with Keeping

It was boiling-hot weather. The tall old house simmered and seethed in a late heat-wave. The Napper family shared the use of the garden, but today it was shadier and cooler for them to stay indoors, in their basement flat. There they lay about, breathless.

'I wish,' said Eddy, 'I wish –'

'Go on,' said his father. 'Wish for a private swimming-pool, or a private ice-cream fountain, or a private –' He gave up, too hot.

'I wish –' said Eddy, and stopped again.

'Go to the Park, Eddy,' said his mother. 'Ask if the dog upstairs would like a walk, and take him to the Park with you. See friends there. Try the swings for a bit of air.'

'No,' said Eddy. 'I wish I could make a Christmas pudding.'

His parents stared at him, too stupefied by heat to be properly amazed. He said: 'I know you always buy our Christmas pudding, Mum, but we could make one. It wouldn't be too early to make one now. We could. I wish we could.'

'Now?' said his mother faintly. 'In all this heat? And why? The bought puddings have always been all right, haven't they?'

'I remember,' said Mr Napper, 'my granny always made her own Christmas puddings. Always.'

'You and your granny!' said Mrs Napper.

'She made several at once. I remember them boiling away in her kitchen for hours and hours and hours. She made them early and stored them. When Christmas came, she served a pudding kept from the year before.' He sighed, smacked his lips. 'A Christmas pudding improves with keeping.'

Mrs Napper had closed her eyes, apparently in sleep; but Eddy was listening.

'We used to help with the puddings,' said Mr Napper. 'We all had a turn at stirring the mixture. You wished as you stirred, but you mustn't say what your wish was. And the wish came true before the next Christmas.'

'Yes,' cried Eddy. 'That's it! I want to stir and to wish – to wish – '

'Well,' said his mother with her eyes shut, 'if we ever make our own Christmas pudding, it won't be during a heat-wave.'

'I just wish – ' Eddy began again.

'Stop it, Eddy!' said his mother, waking up to be sharp. 'Go to the Park. Here's money for ice-cream.'

When Eddy had gone, his father said: 'That settled him!'

His mother said: 'The ideas they get! Come and gone in a minute, though . . .' They both dozed off.

2

But the idea that had come to Eddy did not go. Not at all.

The Nappers had moved into their basement flat in the spring of that year. Once, long before, the whole house had been one home for one well-off family, with servants, or a servant, in the basement kitchen. Later the house had been split up into flats, one floor to a flat, for separate families. Nowadays one family lived on the first floor, where the bedrooms had been. Another family lived on the ground floor, where the parlour and dining-room had been. (And this family owned a dog, and shared the garden with the Nappers.) And the Nappers themselves lived in the basement.

The conversion of the house into flats had been done many years before, but this was the first time since then – although the Nappers were not to know it – that a child had lived in the basement. Eddy was that child.

Ever since they'd moved into the basement, Eddy had had strange dreams. One dream, rather, and not a dream that his dreaming eyes saw, but something that he dreamt he heard. The sound was so slight, so indistinct, that at first even his dreaming self did not really notice it. *Swish – wish – wish!* it went. *Swish – wish – wish!* . . . The dream-sound, even when he came to hear it properly, never woke him up in fright; indeed, it did not frighten him at all. To begin with, he did not even remember it when he woke up.

But – *Swish – wish – wish!* – the sound became more distinct as time passed, more insistent. Never loud, never threatening, however; but coaxing, cajoling, begging – begging and imploring –

'Please,' said Eddy to his mother, 'oh, *please*! It's not a heat-wave now; it's nearly Christmas. And it's Saturday tomorrow: we've got all day. Can't we make our own Christmas pudding tomorrow? Please, please!'

3

'Oh, Eddy! I'm so busy!'

'You mean we can't?' Eddy looked as if he might cry. 'But we must! Oh, Mum, we must!'

'No, Eddy! And when I say no, I mean no!'

That evening, as they sat round the gas fire in their sitting-room, there was an alarming happening: a sudden rattle and clatter that seemed to start from above and come down and end in a crash – a crash not huge but evidently disastrous; and it was unmistakably in their own basement flat, in their own sitting-room.

And yet it wasn't.

Mrs Napper had sprung to her feet with a cry: 'Someone trying to break in!' Her eyes stared at the blank, wall-papered wall from which the crashing sound had seemed to come. There was nothing whatsoever to be seen; and now there was dead silence – except for the frantic barking of the dog upstairs. (The dog had been left on guard while his family went out, and he hadn't liked what he had just heard, any more than the Nappers had.)

Suddenly Eddy rushed to the wall and put his hands flat upon it. 'I wish – ' he cried. 'I wish – '

His father pulled him away. 'If there's anybody – or anything – there,' he said, 'I'll get at him.' He knocked furiously on the wall several times. Then he calmed himself and began rapping and tapping systematically, listening intently for any sound of hollowness, and swearing under his breath at the intrusive barking of the dog upstairs.

'Ah!' he said. 'At last!' He began scrabbling at the wallpaper with his pocket-knife and his finger-nails. Layer upon layer of wallpaper began to be torn away.

'Whatever will the landlord say?' asked Mrs Napper, who had recovered her courage and some of her calm.

Mr Napper said: 'Eddy, get my tool-box. I don't know what may be under here.' While Eddy was gone, Mrs

Napper fetched dust-sheets and spread them out against the mess.

What lay underneath all the ancient wallpapers was a small, squarish wooden door let into the wall at about waist-level: its knob was gone, but Mr Napper prized it open without too much difficulty. The dog upstairs was still barking; and, as soon as the little door was open, the sound came down to them with greater clearness.

With one hand Mr Napper was feeling through the doorway into the blackness inside. 'There's a shaft in here,' he said. 'It's not wide or deep from front to back, but it seems to go right up. I need the torch, Eddy.'

Even as Eddy came back with the torch, Mr Napper was saying cheerfully: 'We've been making a fuss about nothing. Why, this is just an old-fashioned service-lift, from the time our sitting-room was part of a big kitchen.'

'A lift?' Eddy repeated.

'Only a miniature one, for hauling food straight up from the kitchen to the dining-room and bringing the dirty dishes down again. It was worked by hand.'

Mrs Napper had not spoken. Now she said: 'What about all that rattling and the crash?'

Mr Napper was shining his torch into the shaft of the service-lift. 'The ropes for hauling up and down were rotten with age. They gave way at last. Yes, I can see the worn out ends of the cords.'

'But why should they choose to rot and break now?' asked Mrs Napper. 'Why *now*?'

'Why not now?' asked Mr Napper, closing that part of the discussion. He was still peering into the shaft. 'There was something on the service shelf when it fell. There are bits of broken china and – this –'

He brought out from the darkness of the square hole an odd-looking, dried-looking, black-looking object that sat on the palm of his hand like an irregularly shaped large ball.

'Ugh!' said Mrs Napper instantly.

Mr Napper said: 'It's just the remains of a ball of something – a composite ball of something.' He picked at it with a finger-nail. 'Tiny bits all stuck and dried together . . .' He had worried out a fragment, and now he crumbled it in his hand. 'Look!'

Mrs Napper peered reluctantly over his shoulder. 'Well, I must say . . .'

'What is it?' asked Eddy; but suddenly he knew.

His mother had touched the crumblings, and then immediately wiped her fingers on a corner of dust-sheet. 'It looks like old, old sultanas and raisins and things . . .'

'That's what I think,' said Mr Napper. 'It's a plum pudding. 'It *was* a plum pudding.'

Eddy had known: a Christmas pudding.

'But what was it doing there, in that service-lift thing?' asked Mrs Napper. 'Did someone leave it there deliberately or was it just mislaid? Was any of it eaten, do you think?'

'Hard to tell,' said Mr Napper.

'And why did the workmen leave it there when they sealed up the shaft to make the separate flats?' She was worrying at this mystery. 'Perhaps it was between floors and they didn't see it.'

'Or perhaps they didn't like to touch it,' said Eddy.

'Why do you say that?' his mother asked sharply.

'I don't know,' said Eddy.

They cleared up the mess as well as they could. The ancient pudding was wrapped in newspaper and put in the waste-bin under the kitchen sink.

Then it was time for Eddy to go to bed.

That night Eddy dreamt his dream more clearly than ever before. *Swish – wish – wish!* went whatever it was,

6

round and round: *Swish – wish – wish*! In his dream he was dreaming the sound; and in his dream he opened his eyes and looked across a big old shadowy kitchen, past a towering dresser hung with jugs and stacked with plates and dishes on display, past a little wooden door to a service-lift, past a kitchen range with saucepans and a kettle on it –

His gaze reached the big kitchen table. Someone was standing at the table with his back to Eddy: a boy, just of Eddy's age and height, as far as he could tell. In fact, for an instant, Eddy had the strangest dream-sensation that he, Eddy, was standing there at the kitchen table. He, Eddy, was stirring a mixture of something dark and aromatic with a long wooden spoon in a big earthenware mixing-bowl – stirring round and round – stirring, stirring: *Swish – wish – wish … Swish – wish – wish …*

Wish! whispered the wooden spoon as it went round the bowl. *Wish! Wish!* But Eddy did not know what to wish. His not knowing made the boy at the table turn towards him; and when Eddy saw the boy's face, looked into his eyes, he knew. He knew everything, as though he were inside the boy, inside the boy's mind. He knew that this boy lived here in the basement; he was the child of the servant of the house. He helped his mother to cook the food that was put into the service-lift and hauled up to the dining-room upstairs. He helped her to serve the family who ate in the dining-room, and sat at their ease in the parlour, and slept in the comfortable bedrooms above. He hated the family that had to be served. He was filled with hatred as a bottle can be filled with poison.

The boy at the table was stirring a Christmas pudding for the family upstairs, and he was stirring into it his hatred and a wish –

Wish! whispered the wooden spoon. *Wish! Wish!* And the boy at the table smiled at Eddy, a secret and deadly

7

little smile: they were two conspirators, or one boy. Either way, they were wishing, wishing . . .

Someone screamed, and at that Eddy woke; and the screamer was Eddy himself. He tore out of his bed and his bedroom to where he could see a light in the little kitchen of the basement flat. There were his parents, in their dressing-gowns, drinking cups of tea. The kitchen clock said nearly three o'clock in the morning.

Eddy rushed into his mother's arms with a muddled, terrified account of a nightmare about a Christmas pudding. His mother soothed him, and looked over his head to his father. 'You said it was just coincidence that neither of us could sleep tonight for bad dreams. Is Eddy part of the coincidence, too?'

Mr Napper did not answer.

Mrs Napper said: 'That hateful, *hateful* old corpse of a pudding, or whatever it is, isn't going to spend another minute in my home.' She set Eddy aside so that she could go to the waste-bin under the sink.

'I'll take it outside,' said Mr Napper. 'I'll put it into the dustbin outside.' He was already easing his feet into his gardening shoes.

'The dustbin won't be cleared for another five days,' said Mrs Napper.

'Then I'll put it on the bonfire, and I'll burn it in the morning.'

'Without fail?'

'Without fail.'

Mr Napper carried the Christmas pudding, wrapped in old newspaper, out into the garden, and Eddy was sent back to bed by his mother. He lay awake in bed until he heard his father's footsteps coming back from the garden and into the flat. He didn't feel safe until he heard that.

Then he could go to sleep. But even then he slept lightly, anxiously. He heard the first of the cars in the road

8

outside. Then he heard the people upstairs letting their dog out into the garden, as usual. The dog went bouncing and barking away into the distance, as it always did. Then he heard his parents getting up. And then – because he wanted to see the bonfire's first burning – to *witness it* – Eddy got up, too.

So Eddy was with his father when Mr Napper went to light the bonfire. Indeed, Eddy was ahead of him on the narrow path, and he was carrying the box of matches.

'Whereabouts did you put the – the thing?' asked Eddy.

'The plum pudding? I put it on the very top of the bonfire.'

But it was not there. It had gone. There was a bit of crumpled old newspaper, but no pudding. Then Eddy saw why it had gone, and where. It had been dragged down from the top of the bonfire, and now it lay on the ground on the far side of the bonfire, partly eaten; and beside it lay the dog from the ground-floor flat. Eddy knew from the way the dog lay, and the absolute stillness of its body, that the dog was dead.

Mr Napper saw what Eddy saw.

Mr Napper said: 'Don't touch that dog, Eddy. Don't touch anything. I'm going back to tell them what's happened. You can come with me.'

But Eddy stayed by the bonfire because his feet seemed to have grown into the ground, and his father went back by himself. Alone, Eddy began to shiver; he wanted to cry; he wanted to scream. He knew what he wanted to do most of all. With trembling fingers he struck a match and lit the bonfire in several places. The heap was very dry and soon caught: it blazed merrily, forming glowing caves of fire within its heart. Eddy picked up the half-eaten Christmas pudding and flung it into one of the fiery caverns, and blue flames seemed to leap to welcome it and consume it.

Then Eddy began really to cry, and then felt his father's arms round him, holding him, comforting him, and heard the voice of his mother and then the lamentations of the family of the ground-floor flat, whose dog had been poisoned by what it had eaten.

And the bonfire flamed and blazed with flames like the flames of Hell.

Samantha and
the Ghost

This was the first time that Samantha had climbed her grandparents' apple tree, and at the top she found the Ghost. After expressions of surprise on both sides, they settled sociably among the branches.

'Nice to have someone to chat to, for once,' said the Ghost.

'But oughtn't you to be groaning or clanking chains?' asked Samantha.

'I'm not the groaning kind, and I haven't chains to clank,' said the Ghost. 'Although I do have something else, for moonlit nights.'

'What?'

But the Ghost slid away from that point; he was evasive. All that Samantha could see of him in the sunlight was a wide shimmer of air over one of the outermost apple branches. If she looked directly, she could hardly be sure that he was there at all. If she focused her gaze to one side on (say) the chimney-pots of her grandparents' bungalow, then – out of the corner of her eye – she could see him more clearly. Not his face, not his clothing, but an impression of a wide body and limbs. His hands seemed to be resting on his knees: was he holding something across them?

'I've never thought of an apple tree being haunted,' Samantha remarked. She remembered something: 'My grandfather says this tree never bears any fruit, never has any blossom even. He says it's unnatural. Well, perhaps it's because you live here.'

'Possibly,' said the Ghost, not interested. Samantha thought he would be interested all right if she revealed to him that her grandfather was seriously thinking of cutting down this unsatisfactory tree to make room for raspberry canes. But she decided not to tell him that.

The Ghost said: 'This tree is not my real haunt – not my original one. I was already haunting here when it was planted. You see, my bedchamber, where I first began to haunt, was here.'

'Here?'

'*Here*, where the top of this apple tree now is. Our mansion was ten times the size of any of these low cottages' (he meant the bungalows, Samantha realized), 'and it stood handsomely where they have now been built. My bedchamber, naturally, was on the first floor, at exactly this level: here – *here*.' The ghostly shimmer moved around in the top of the apple tree and beyond it, apparently pacing out the dimensions of a long-ago bedroom.

'And the mansion has gone – completely gone?' Samantha asked wonderingly.

'I suppose I overhaunted it,' the Ghost admitted. 'I made life impossible for the inhabitants.'

'But if you don't groan or clank chains or anything . . .'

'I didn't say I didn't do *anything*.' The shimmer was seated again, and the hands moved – yes, holding something. 'At first I haunted thoroughly – much more thoroughly than I have ever had the heart to do since – I haunted that house to the top of my ability. Nobody could go on living in it. Nobody. Soon the house stood empty, neglected. Woodworm abounded; dry rot set in. In the end, the thing had to be pulled down completely, razed to the ground, to make room for lesser dwellings.'

'Leaving you stranded in mid-air,' said Samantha.

'Exactly. Most awkward. There must be quite a few unfortunate spirits in my plight, up and down the country.' (Samantha suddenly remembered a piercingly cold pool of air always to be passed through on a certain staircase of her school: an old ghost built into a new building, perhaps?)

The Ghost was going on: 'I can tell you, I was glad when the apple tree grew up to bedchamber level. Something solid to put my feet up on at last.'

'Why do you haunt a bedroom?' asked Samantha.

'I was a permanent invalid.'

'I'm so sorry.' Samantha had quite a tender heart. 'Not bedridden though?'

'Not entirely, but confined to the bedchamber,' the Ghost sighed. 'I died there.'

A sad little silence, in which they heard from below the sound of the opening of the french windows of the bungalow. Samantha's grandmother stepped into the garden: 'Samantha!' She looked all round, but not upwards, and Samantha made no sound. 'Tea, Samantha!' She added enticingly: 'And something special for tea!' She did not wait for an answer, partly because she was rather deaf, and knew it. She went back indoors, confident of Samantha's following her.

'What's special for tea?' the Ghost asked eagerly.

'I think it'll be fried sausage and bacon today.' Samantha was already beginning to clamber down the tree. She paused to sniff the air: 'Yes, sausage and bacon.'

The Ghost was also sniffing, in a different way. He was crying, Samantha realized. Between sobs he whimpered: 'Fried sausages and bacon! How I used to adore fried sausages and bacon! Bacon all curled and crisp, and sausages bursting out of their little weskits . . .'

Samantha had no idea how you comforted a ghost or lent one a handkerchief. And she hadn't a handkerchief anyway; and she was not really sure how sympathetic she felt towards a shimmer crying its heart out over fried sausages and bacon; and her tea was waiting for her . . .

She hardened her heart against the Ghost, and jumped the last few feet to the ground. She heard, from behind her and above, the Ghost's pleading: 'Come again – please, come again . . .'

She went indoors.

After tea, Samantha spent the evening as usual with her grandparents, watching TV and playing cards. When they played, the room seemed very quiet, except for the wind moaning in the chimney and shrieking and screeching round the bungalow. 'The wind's up again,' said Samantha. 'Like last night.'

Her grandmother went on counting knitting stitches, but her grandfather began his usual complaint. He was not really a grumbler, Samantha knew, but the sound of the wind got on his nerves. He said so. 'It's a ghastly sound,' he said, 'and it's against all reason and nature. How can the wind wail and moan and shriek *when there isn't any wind*? Time and time again, when that row starts, I've gone outside, and the air is still – still. It's unnatural.'

'Unnatural,' Samantha repeated to herself, and remembered the barrenness of the apple tree, and remembered the Ghost ... Suddenly it dawned upon her that almost certainly she knew what object the Ghost held in his hands. She flushed with indignation.

The next morning she climbed the apple tree and tackled the Ghost. 'You may not have chains to clank, but you have a violin and you play it at night: you play it shockingly, *horribly* badly, don't you?'

The Ghost actually seemed pleased. 'So you heard my fiddling last night?'

'We couldn't help hearing you. You made my grandfather's evening a misery. Need you?'

'It's a very important part of the haunt,' the Ghost said.

Before she could stop him, he had tucked the misty instrument into position under his misty chin and had drawn the bow across the strings. A long thin screech tore the morning quiet. Down in the bungalow garden. Samantha's grandfather dropped his trowel with an exclamation of agony and clapped his hands to his ears.

'I'm sure you've no right to do that in the daytime,' Samantha said sternly to the Ghost. 'And why do it at all?'

'I played in life. I must do so after death.'

'But why? I mean, why did you play in life? You play so abominably, you can't ever have enjoyed it.'

'No,' said the Ghost. 'But I didn't mind it. I'm not in the least musical, you see.'

'Then why – *why* – '

'I was an invalid. I needed constant attention. Constant. But after some years I found that people were losing interest in me; they were beginning to neglect to answer my bell. That's when I got myself a fiddle and began fiddling. Oh my! They came soon enough then!' He

15

chuckled. 'They rushed to beg me to stop. I got into the habit of fiddling instead of ringing the bell.'

Samantha was looking at the Ghost with new eyes. 'What was your illness?' she asked.

Again the Ghost was pleased. 'Nobody knew, ever. The doctors, one and all, were baffled. Every medicine and drug and linctus and embrocation and inhalant and tablet and pill – they tried everything. In vain, in vain.'

'What were the symptoms of the illness?'

'Difficult to define,' said the Ghost. 'Certainly lassitude.'

'Lassitude?'

'Well, lethargy.'

'Lethargy?'

'Don't repeat so, dear girl! Manners, manners! Yes, lassitude and lethargy: the mere notion of activity, work of any description, produced faintness, prostration, collapse. So, lassitude, lethargy –'

'Laziness,' Samantha said under her breath.

'I beg your pardon?'

'Nothing. How old were you when you died?'

'A medical triumph, I suppose: I was eighty-nine. A frail eighty-nine, of course.'

'How much did you weigh?'

'I really cannot see what – seventeen stone, actually.'

Samantha drew a deep breath. She shouted: 'You were a great, fat, lazy old pig!'

The Ghost shimmered violently with anger. 'You're an ill-bred, uppish, rude little girl!'

Samantha disregarded him as though he had not spoken. 'You're selfish and unkind and you've just got to stop making my grandfather's life a misery with your horrible fiddling!'

'Who says?'

'I say!'

They glared at each other.

'Get out of my tree!' said the Ghost.

'Your tree!'

'As long as my bedchamber is at the top!'

'I wouldn't stay anywhere near your silly bedroom or your stupid violin or your idiotic seventeen stone – so there!' And Samantha slid rapidly down through the branches to the ground and ran indoors. Nor did she emerge again.

That evening the screaming and shrieking round the bungalow reached an almost unbelievable pitch. Even Samantha's deaf grandmother seemed to notice it, and her grandfather grew very pale.

Samantha flung down her hand of cards, and shouted: 'You'll have to move house, won't you?'

'No, dear,' said her grandmother.

'No,' said her grandfather. 'At our age, on our pensions, we can't afford to move house all over again.'

'And perhaps we'll cut down the apple tree next spring,' said Grandmother, 'and perhaps that'll make a difference. Wind whistles through trees.'

'This isn't wind,' said Grandfather.

'I'm glad you'll cut the tree down, anyway,' Samantha declared with savagery.

'But only if the poor thing still doesn't have any fruit blossom next spring,' said her grandmother.

They resumed their cards, playing with stony determination. Then Samantha went to bed, where she fell asleep at last to the infuriated raging of a badly played violin.

The next day was the last of Samantha's visit. Deliberately she went nowhere near the apple tree. She and her grandmother went by bus to the shops. Gently it rained.

That night they all went to bed early. There had been only a little moaning and wailing down the chimney, nothing violent. To Samantha's surprise, even this sound had died to silence. She wondered why.

Late into the night Samantha stayed awake, wondering. Almost, she was worrying. At last she got up, put on her dressing-gown and tiptoed through the bungalow to the french windows and out.

There was the apple tree, sharply defined in the moonlight, and there was the Ghost. By moonlight he and his ghostly surroundings were much more visible. He seemed to be leaning out of a window at the top of the apple tree. He was looking down at her. She was taken aback. He was, indeed, grossly fat, and very old, too, with floating white hair; but he had a babyish look which, without being exactly attractive, was at least pitiful.

'Please,' he whispered down to her, 'please – please come up ...' Samantha had, of course, been warned against strangers with strange invitations, but this one was still not very much more than a shimmer up a tree. He was no danger. She climbed up to him and they sat together, as they had done on that first, friendly afternoon, talking. Samantha perched on a branch; the Ghost, in a long, flowered dressing-gown, sat in his rocking-chair by an open fire, which gave out an uncosy blaze. Round the Ghost, foggily, Samantha could see the bedchamber itself: tall windows, one of them still open; a four-poster bed; and a table whose top was crammed with medicine bottles and old-fashioned pillboxes.

'You didn't visit me today,' the Ghost said reproachfully.

'I thought we'd quarrelled.'

'My dear girl, in life I was used to quarrels. What I never got used to – can never get used to – is being alone. Loneliness ...' He shed tears.

With an effort Samantha said: 'I'm sorry.'

'You'll visit me again tomorrow?'

'I'm afraid not. I'm going home tomorrow morning.'

He burst into sobs.

Samantha could contain herself no longer. '*You* cry because you have to put up with not having a visitor, but what about my poor grandfather who has to put up with your awful, awful fiddling night after night? What about that?'

'I'd stop playing – I'd stop playing for ever,' wailed the Ghost, 'if only I didn't have to haunt here alone, all alone. Alone for hundreds and hundreds of years . . .'

'I'm sorry,' Samantha repeated. 'I go home tomorrow.'

The Ghost said wistfully, 'Do you think anyone else will ever climb this apple tree for a chat?'

'No.'

'No?'

'Because my grandfather's going to have it chopped down next spring unless it has blossom then. And it won't do that as long as you stay here, will it?'

'I can see what you're hinting at,' said the Ghost. 'You think I should leave.'

Samantha said nothing.

'But how could I leave this?' He waved his arm around the misty bedroom. 'I'm not fond of it, but it's all I have of home.'

'Do you know,' said Samantha, 'you're not only a ghost, but you're haunting the mere ghost of a bedroom? That's not worthy of you.'

'Isn't it?'

'No. If I were you, I'd get away. I'd go.'

'But where could I go?'

'Places,' Samantha said crisply.

'Have a good time, you mean? But *alone*?'

'Not alone. You said there must be lots of ghosts like yourself, stranded in mid-air, made more or less homeless.

Go and find them. Join up with them. Make up a party, and go places.'

'Really?' He was becoming excited. 'Cut a dash?'

'That's it. Leave this dreary ghost of a room and all this dreary rubbish.' Samantha reached forward and swept her hand dramatically over the surface of the medicine table; but her hand went through it all without effect, leaving it undisturbed.

'Allow me!' The Ghost heaved himself from his chair and waddled the few steps towards the table. He was carrying his violin in his left hand, the bow in his right. With vicious dabs of his bow, the Ghost sent bottles and boxes flying off the table in an irregular rain of medication. Samantha saw that not one of them reached the floor, because they melted into nothingness even as they fell.

The Ghost threw the bow after the bottles and boxes, and that vanished too.

A few more waddling steps, and the Ghost was at the window. With surprising agility, he clambered up, stood on the sill –

Samantha gasped at the peril of it; but then – what peril to a ghost?

'Never again!' cried the Ghost, and flung the violin from him in a great arc. For a moment Samantha saw its shape in the moonlight; then it faded, vanished.

'And I'm off!' The Ghost flung himself forward through the window: he did not fall, he did not fly, and he certainly did not vanish. He went. He hurried through the air until he was lost to Samantha's sight. Pleasure-seeking.

Samantha was left at the top of the apple tree. Round her, every trace of that ghostly bedroom had vanished with the going of the Ghost himself. She climbed down and went to bed.

The next day Samantha went home. She wrote to her

grandparents to thank them for her visit; and in time she had a letter back. They reported that, oddly, the screeches and moanings round the house and down the chimney had stopped.

Samantha nodded to herself.

In the spring she visited the bungalow again. The apple tree was full of fruit blossom – a picture, as Samantha's grandmother said – and there was no question now of chopping it down.

That autumn the tree bore its first crop – a bumper one. Samantha went to help pick the apples. Her grandfather was not allowed to climb ladders, so Samantha climbed and picked. She climbed to the very top of the tree, and perched there for a moment.

'What's it like up there?' called her grandfather, from below.

'Nice,' said Samantha. 'But a bit lonely.'

A Prince in Another Place

I was caretaker at our school at the time; but I was not –
I repeat, *not* – responsible for the damage done to the
school playground. People said the asphalt looked as if it
had boiled up under quite extraordinary heat: how could
I be held responsible for that?

I'll begin at the beginning, and the beginning was when
poor young Mr Hartley hanged himself.

Mr Hartley was one of the three teachers at Little
Pawley Church of England Primary School: the other two
were Mr Ezra Bryce, the headmaster, and Mrs Salt, in
charge of Infants. The Vicar, old Mr Widdington, came
into school sometimes to help with Assembly and Reli-
gious Instruction.

Mr Hartley was very young, very timid and very
inexperienced – and he had just recovered from an illness, I
believe. This was his first teaching job and – as it turned

out – his last. Mr Bryce did for him. Mr Bryce bullied him and harried him and sneered at him and jeered at him and altogether made Mr Hartley's life so appalling (as only Mr Bryce knew how) that the poor young man decided to leave it. He committed suicide in his lodgings on the second day of his second term at the school.

Of course, anyone in the village could make a good guess at what lay behind that death; but Bully Bryce was sly as well as a bully, and he could always cover up after himself. At different times the police and the Education people came round asking questions, but he was able to explain everything. He said that poor young Hartley had been far too highly strung to be a teacher – and he was in delicate health, too. So, in spite of all the fatherly support that he – Mr Bryce – had tried to give him, the young man had cracked under the strain. Such a pity, said Mr Bryce. (I can imagine the tears coming to his eyes as he spoke.)

After the inquest, the funeral took place far away, in Mr Hartley's home parish. His only family was a widowed mother and an elder brother, who came home from abroad for the funeral. That seemed to be the end of Mr Hartley.

The day after the funeral, a new teacher turned up at the school to take over Mr Hartley's work there. This was Mr Dickins. He was just a stopgap, of course – a supply teacher sent by the Education people; he wouldn't be staying long, he said. For a teacher, he was rather a remarkable-looking man. He had a head of really flaming red hair; and he smiled to himself a good deal, and, when he laughed, you saw he had excellent teeth, strong-looking and rather pointed, almost sharp. He had very small feet. I must have said something about them to him once – he was an easy chap, and often had a word with me. I remember he said he had the greatest difficulty in getting shoes to fit – 'the trouble is my odd-shaped feet, Mr Jackson,' he said. But at least he was nimble enough, as far as I could see.

At first, everyone wondered how the new teacher would stand up to his headmaster. For, indeed, it was possible to stand up to Bully Bryce. Mrs Salt, of Infants, had been doing it for years, by being deaf as a post whenever her headmaster addressed her; and she defended her Infants as a tigress defends her cubs. And the Juniors were able to look after themselves, chiefly by banding together in self-defence. I've heard them chanting outside the headmaster's window:

> Bully B, Bully B,
> My dad will come
> If you touch me!

As for me, I could stand up to Mr Bryce – or I wouldn't have been school caretaker for so long. But if I'd been young and frightened, like poor Mr Hartley – oh, there's no doubt of it: Mr Bryce knew how to pick his victims.

But it was soon plain that Mr Dickins wouldn't need to stand up to Mr Bryce: he became his friend instead – his bosom friend. They were always together: in school hours they consulted together, and took their cups of tea and their dinners together. In the evening, they would go for a drink together in the pub.

For some reason, old Mr Widdington, the Vicar, became very much upset at this friendship. He was worrying about it one day when he met me in the village street: 'And there's another thing, Mr Jackson,' he said. 'Is this Mr Dickins really suitable as a teacher, even for a short time? You've a grandchild in the Juniors: what does she say?'

'Well, Vicar,' I said, 'I think our Susie quite enjoys being taught by him.'

'We must look for more than *pleasure*,' he says, shaking his reverend grey locks. He was an old-fashioned chap in his ideas. 'What does he *teach* them?'

'The usual things, I suppose,' I said, 'even if he teaches them in these unusual, funny ways they do nowadays.'

'Unusual? Funny?' Mr Widdington said quite sharply. 'What do you mean?'

'Well, Susie says her class were doing number-work or arithmetic or new maths or whatever they call it nowadays. Mr Dickins wanted to show them five and five. So he lit all the fingers and thumb of one hand, like candles. And then, with his flaming fingers and thumb, he lit all the fingers and thumb of his other hand, so that he had five and five – ten candles.'

After a little pause, Mr Widdington said: 'That was a conjuring trick.'

'I suppose it must have been,' I said.

'Anything else?' asked Mr Widdington.

'Well, Susie says he's told them that he's really a Prince in another place.'

'Where?'

'He didn't say. In another place. Those were his words, according to Susie. But I said to Susie: "He can't be one of our princes from Buckingham Palace, and there aren't many princes about elsewhere, as there used to be, even abroad."'

'I don't like it,' said Mr Widdington. '"A Prince in another place" – no, I don't like it at all. I shall get in touch with the Education Authority to check up on the man's background and qualifications.'

(I thought to myself, And a nice long time that'll take!)

'And in the meantime,' said Mr Widdington, 'I shall make a point of having a private word with Mr Bryce about his Mr Dickins.'

'You'll be lucky, Vicar,' I said. 'You'll find it hard to

get Bryce without Dickins – it's like a man and his shadow nowadays.'

'I'll get Bryce to come into the church for a chat,' says the Vicar. The church and the churchyard are right next to the school, with only a wall between them and a door in the wall.

I don't know why the Vicar thought he could get Mr Bryce into the church without Mr Dickins coming too: the plan didn't seem a particularly good one to me. But the Vicar thought it was, and – oddly – he was proved right.

The next day, just after school, the Vicar caught Mr Bryce and asked him to come into the church to look at some arrangements there for the next children's Harvest Festival. Mr Bryce could be quite obliging, if it suited him, and he agreed to go at once. 'Coming, Nick?' he said over his shoulder to Mr Dickins. Mr Dickins hesitated for a moment, then followed them through the door into the churchyard.

I pretended to be clearing rubbish in the playground, so that I could watch the three of them over the wall.

They were going through the churchyard by a path so narrow that you could only walk single-file. Mr Widdington led the way, and Mr Dickins came last; and Mr Bryce was in the middle, between the two of them. They rounded the corner of the church and so came to the main south door. Mr Widdington was just leading the way into the church, and Mr Bryce following, when I heard Mr Dickins give a cry of pain; and they turned back to him. I couldn't hear what was said, but it was plain from the tones of voice and the gestures that Mr Dickins had twisted his ankle or hurt it in some way. He wanted to rest it, while the other two went into the church. So they went in, and he stayed outside, sitting on one tombstone with his foot up on another.

I was watching Mr Dickins, but I didn't realize that he was also watching me. He never missed much. Now he waved to me in a very cheery way from his tombstone. I had the feeling that, if I'd been near enough, I should have seen him wink.

Mr Widdington and Mr Bryce were a long time talking in the church, but I don't think the talk went the way that Mr Widdington had hoped. When they came out of the church, they didn't come out together. Mr Bryce burst out first and rushed up to Mr Dickins, as if he'd been longing to get back to him. He seized him by the hand and hauled him to his feet, paying no attention to the hurt done to Mr Dickins's ankle – and really it didn't seem as if there could ever have been much wrong with it, anyway. They went striding off together, the two of them, arm in arm; and, a little later, the Vicar came shuffling out of the church. He looked his age then – old, and dejected. Somehow, defeated. Yes, as if he'd failed.

And now Mr Bryce and Mr Dickins seemed closer than ever. They took to staying on at the school, after the children and Mrs Salt had gone home, and Mr Dickins would play his fiddle. He may have played well, but his tunes were strange, and I didn't like to hear them.

And now I noticed that Susie and her friends had a new little ditty for playtime. They'd dance in a ring and chant:

> *Bully B, Bully B,*
> *Where are you going*
> *And what do you see?*

It wasn't just a few children either. That nonsense chant became a kind of craze. All the children were singing the same song in playtime, dancing round in rings of five or six or seven. The playground was giddy with the whirling and singing. Once I saw Mr Bryce at his window staring out on it all, and, at his elbow, just behind him, Mr Dickins smiling quietly to himself, as usual.

All this was in the summer term. The weather was fine, dry, but there was no sultriness, no hint of storms building up. Yet perhaps there was a strange feeling in the air – or was I just imagining it? Certainly old Widdington was fussing more than usual, and more anxiously. He dropped into the school almost every day now, on one excuse or another. The dancing and singing of the children in the playground worried him. Why did they do it? he asked. He got me to ask Susie that – where the words and the dancing came from, who started it, or who had taught them all. But Susie didn't know. She said they had all just begun doing it; that was all.

I told Mr Widdington what Susie had said, and he looked even more upset. I said, 'Well, have you had an answer to that letter you wrote to the Education people about Mr Dickins?'

'Not yet. But I've also written to – to someone else.'

I didn't want to seem inquisitive. As it turned out, I learnt soon enough who *someone else* was.

Playtime was just over that day. The rings of dancing, singing children had broken up; they were all going back to their classrooms. I had been by the school gate, watching them. I heard footsteps coming up behind me, but I paid no attention. Then a voice: 'Excuse me. Is Mr Widdington about?'

And the voice was the voice of poor young Mr Hartley, that killed himself . . .

I turned round because I was too frightened not to, if you see what I mean, and there was Mr Hartley looking at me! For two awful seconds that's what I thought, and then I realized that this man was very like our Mr Hartley, but older, more solid-looking, and sunburnt from foreign lands. He could see what I had been thinking. He said: 'I

28

am the brother of Timothy Hartley, who used to teach here, and you must be Mr Jackson.' We shook hands. He explained that the Vicar had asked him to meet him here; he was a little early. Then he said: 'Mr Widdington has asked me to see Mr Bryce, to talk to him.'

I said: 'If it's for the sake of your poor brother, Mr Hartley, it'll be a waste of your breath. It will, really.'

'It's not for his sake; it's for Mr Bryce's own sake.'

I could only stare at him. He went on: 'Mr Jackson, I would never, never have consented to come here to see this man, except that your Mr Widdington asked me to – implored me to. He said the matter was very urgent indeed.' I still stared at Mr Hartley; and now he looked aside in an embarrassed way, and said: 'Mr Widdington mentioned Mr Bryce's immortal soul.'

From the school, the fiddle-playing of Mr Dickins had started up; Mr Dickins had never played his tunes in school hours before.

The elder Mr Hartley heard the fiddling. He said: 'I'm not waiting for Mr Widdington, after all. I'm going to Mr Bryce now. Now.'

'Through that door, then,' I said, and pointed across the playground.

When he had gone into the school, everything was very quiet and still, except for the fiddling: that went on for a while. Then the door from the churchyard into the playground clicked, and I looked that way and saw the Vicar coming through. He hesitated on the edge of the playground, looking round him. I was just going over to him, when things began to happen.

The school door through which Mr Hartley had gone opened again, and he came out. He had not looked to me a man to be easily scared, but now his face was chalky-white, his eyes were staring, and he walked altogether like a sleepwalker in a nightmare. He came across the deserted playground towards the gate, and I came forward a little to meet him.

Behind him, in the doorway, appeared Mr Bryce. His face was dark, and he was shouting foul abuse after Mr Hartley – abuse not only of him but also of the poor young man who had hanged himself. And behind Mr Bryce smiled the face of Mr Dickins.

Mr Bryce stood in the doorway, nearly filling it, for he was a big man. I've not yet told you what he looked like. Bullies can be fat or thin or medium-sized: Bully Bryce was the heavy, bull-like kind. He filled his clothes almost to bursting, and his head seemed to have burst up out of his collar, and his eyes seemed to be bursting from his head. They were bloodshot eyes, as well as bulging, and they glared now; and when he bellowed his abuse across the playground, the spittle flew from his mouth at every word.

Mr Hartley had reached me, and I was partly supporting him while he tried to recover himself. So we stood on the edge of the playground, and I was facing it. Mr Hartley had his back to it at first, but pretty soon he turned his head to see what was fixing my attention. And the Vicar too, also on the edge of the playground, was staring; and Mrs Salt, of the Infants, now stood in her doorway to the playground, gazing distractedly and crying: 'Children! Children! Stop, stop!'

For all the children of the school were coming out on to the playground. The Infants were climbing out of the low windows of their classroom, one after another, and holding hands as they danced away across the playground, while Mrs Salt called to them in vain: 'Whatever are you doing? Stop, stop!' The Juniors, too, had come streaming out of the building and, hand in hand, ran and danced and joined up with the Infants in one long skein of children that moved to and fro in ceaseless meander over the playground.

Now Mr Bryce was advancing into the playground, always with Mr Dickins at his elbow. At first I thought he was coming to put a stop to what was going on, but this was not so. He had stopped storming and shouting; he was quite silent. He walked slowly, perhaps reluctantly, step after step, into the middle of the playground, and the skein of dancing children kept clear of him as he moved. I saw that Mr Dickins had tucked his fiddle under one arm, and now had the other hooked into Mr Bryce's. They were arm in arm, as so often, but this time they were not walking equally: Mr Dickins was urging Mr Bryce forward, positively pulling him along. They reached the middle of the playground, and went no further. And the children were running mazily about them, chanting now:

> Bully B, Bully B,
> Where are you going
> And what do you see?

The long line of children wavered about the playground until the two ends of it came together, and joined. Suddenly there was one irregularly shaped ring of children with Mr Bryce and Mr Dickins in the middle of it.

The children still ran; and, as they ran, they pulled outwards – outwards – to form a proper circle round the two men. When they had achieved this, more or less, they stopped running and changed to dancing on the spot, still chanting as they danced:

> Bully B, Bully B,
> Where are you going
> And what do you see?

And the air in the playground seemed to tighten, so that

there was hardly room to breathe; and we, the witnesses –
the Vicar, Mr Hartley, Mrs Salt, and myself – stood stock-
still and staring –

> *Bully B, Bully B,*
> *Where are you going*
> *And what –*

– and there was a sound such as I hope never to hear
again on earth: a deafening CRACK! and at the same
time an upward burst of flaming light against which –
instantaneously – my eyes closed. But on the inside of my
eyelids was printed the image of Mr Dickins and Mr
Bryce, entwined, and they seemed to be all on fire inside
my eyelids, and I heard a howl that was more than any
human being could make, and yet it was human, and I
knew that it had been made by Mr Bryce.

I put my hands up to my shut eyes, as though I had
been blinded, and I fell to my knees.

When I opened my eyes again, the playground was in
confusion. The children were no longer holding hands,
or dancing, or chanting; they ran aimlessly, or stood, or
sat, some sobbing or weeping, others laughing hysteri-
cally. Mrs Salt was trying to control them and get them
back to their classrooms. The Vicar was leaning against
the wall of the churchyard, as though he had been
flattened there by the blast of an explosion. Mr Hartley
was lying on the ground beside me, half out of his senses
for the time being.

The middle of the playground was empty: no Mr Bryce,
no Mr Dickins. Where they had stood, there was a huge,
bubbled scar in the asphalt, like two lips that had opened
widely once – perhaps to swallow some tasty morsel –
and then closed again in a dreadful sneer.

That's really all. Mr Bryce and Mr Dickins were never
seen again. Nobody knew where they'd gone. Mrs Salt

said they couldn't just have vanished, as we seemed to think: that was against common sense and reason. She was sure they'd slipped away, under our very noses, and escaped abroad to an Enemy Power, for whom they had been spying in this country.

'An Enemy Power . . .' Mr Widdington said thoughtfully.

We had trouble with the Education people. They had never answered Mr Widdington's letter because they hadn't been able to trace Mr Dickins in their records. Certainly, they had never sent us a Mr Dickins as a supply teacher. They denounced Mr Dickins as an impostor.

When they heard of the mysterious disappearance of two of our staff – well, one, because, of course, they wouldn't count Mr Dickins – they went so far as to send an official in person to make inquiries. He found out no more than I've already told you, but, just before he was leaving, he noticed the damage in the playground. He said to me: 'What the Hell's been going on here?'

I didn't answer him. I didn't think that kind of language was suitable for an Education person in a primary school playground; I wouldn't have liked Susie to hear him.

Black Eyes

Cousin Lucinda was coming to stay with Jane, just for the weekend.

Jane had never met Lucinda, but Jane's mother said she was a year younger than Jane, and they must all be very kind to her. Jane imagined the rest. She imagined a shy little girl with blue eyes and golden curls that bobbed about a round, rosy face. She would be rather cuddly, and they would play with their teddy-bears together.

But Lucinda was not at all like that. She was thin, and her hair was black without any curl to it, and her eyes were black in a white face – eyes as black as the Pontefract cakes you find in a liquorice assortment. Jane didn't like liquorice.

And Lucinda's teddy-bear had black eyes, too.

'He was exactly like your teddy-bear to begin with,' said Lucinda, 'with eyes exactly like yours. But then one day my teddy-bear saw something so horrid – so *horrible* – that his eyes dropped out. Then my mother made black eyes for him, with black wool.' She paused for a quick breath. 'But his eyes aren't made of ordinary black wool, and they're not stitched in an ordinary way. The black wool is magic, and my mother is a witch.'

Jane said feebly, 'My mother says your mother is her sister, so she can't be a witch.'

'That's what your mother would like to believe,' said Lucinda.

The two little girls were in their nightdresses, in Jane's room, which Lucinda was sharing for two nights. They had been playing and talking before going to bed.

Jane's father came in to say good-night. He caught sight of the two teddies lying side by side. Lucinda's teddy never wore any clothes, she said; and Jane had just undressed her teddy for the night, taking off the trousers and jersey and balaclava helmet, with holes for the ears, that her mother had once knitted for him. So the two teddies lay side by side, with nothing on, and Jane's father cried: 'Twins! Twin teddy-bears – as like as two apples in a bowl!'

(He did not notice the difference in their eyes: that was the kind of thing he would never notice.)

He darted forward, snatched up each teddy-bear by a leg and began juggling with them – throwing them up, one after the other, very quickly, and catching them as quickly, so that there were always two teddy-bears whirling round in the air. He sometimes juggled with apples like this, until Jane's mother told him to stop before he dropped one and bruised it.

Both the little girls were jumping about and shouting to him to stop, as he meant them to. But Lucinda's shouts turned into screams and then into long, screeching sobs.

Jane's father stopped at once and thrust both teddy-bears into her arms and tried to hug her and kiss her and talk to her gently, saying over and over again that he hadn't hurt the teddies one bit – they'd *liked* it – and he was very, very sorry. But Lucinda wriggled away from him and threw Jane's teddy away, hard, so that it hit the bedroom wall with a smack; and she went on sobbing.

In the end, Jane's father left them. You could see that he was really upset.

Lucinda stopped crying. She said: 'Sorry! He'll be sorry!'

'What do you mean?' asked Jane.

'Didn't you see the look my teddy gave your father out of his magic black eyes?'

'No,' said Jane. 'My teddy-bear likes my father, even when he throws him up into the air. And my teddy can look at him better than your teddy, because my teddy has *real* teddy eyes. I don't believe your teddy can look at all with woolwork eyes. Not as well as my teddy, anyway.'

'Your teddy has silly eyes,' said Lucinda. 'Yours is a silly teddy. Silly Teddy, Silly Teddy – that's your teddy's name now.'

'No, it isn't,' said Jane.

'Yes, it is,' said Lucinda. 'And my teddy is called Black Teddy. And your father will be sorry that he threw Black Teddy up into the air, so that Black Teddy had to look at him with his magic eyes.'

Jane wanted to say something back, but her mother came in, rather anxiously, having heard about the juggling. She made the little girls get into their beds at once, and then she tucked them up, and kissed them goodnight, and went out, turning off the light.

They did not speak again. Perhaps Lucinda went quickly to sleep – Jane did not know. Jane herself burrowed under the bedclothes and then whispered in her teddy's ear: 'I don't like Black Teddy, do you? But he's not staying long . . .'

The next morning, after breakfast, Jane's father was washing up when he broke a cup.

'Oh, really!' said his wife.

'It's only one of the cheap ones,' he said.

'There isn't such a thing as a cheap cup,' she retorted. 'If you go on breaking cups, I can't let you wash up.'

'I'm planning to break the whole set,' said Jane's father.

And no more was said, but Lucinda whispered to Jane, 'Black Teddy did that.'

'Did what?'

'Made him break that cup. Black Teddy ill-wished him to do it with a look from his magic eyes.'

'I don't believe it.'

'Oh, Black Teddy can easily do that. He's ill-wished my father so that he's broken something, and my mother's got angry, and then my father's got angry, and then they've both screamed and screamed at each other, and broken more things; and Black Teddy ill-wished it all with his magic eyes. Just as he ill-wished your father.'

Jane wanted to shout: 'I don't believe it!' But she was afraid of what Lucinda might say back. She was afraid of Lucinda, or of Black Teddy. So she just turned away.

That Saturday morning Jane's mother took the little girls out with her when she went shopping. Jane said it would be better if they left their teddy-bears at home, each on a separate bed. So they did.

When they got home, Jane went to her room to make sure that her teddy-bear was all right. He sat exactly as she had left him, she thought, fully dressed – but then she saw that his balaclava helmet was on back to front. She trembled with anger as she put it right.

Lucinda had come into the room just behind her. 'You

did that!' said Jane. 'You turned his balaclava round so that he couldn't see.'

'He can't see, anyway, with those silly eyes,' said Lucinda. 'And I didn't touch him. Black Teddy just ill-wished it to happen to him, and it did.'

'It wasn't Black Teddy; it was you!' said Jane. 'And my teddy can see except when his balaclava's on back to front.'

'Your silly teddy can't see, ever. But Black Teddy, if he wanted to – Black Teddy could see through the back of a balaclava helmet, and through doors, and through walls; he can see through everything when he wants to ill-wish with his magic eyes.'

Jane stamped her foot and shouted: 'Go away!'

Lucinda said: 'I'm going away tomorrow morning and I'm never coming back. You hate me.'

Jane said: 'Yes, I hate you!'

At that moment, Jane's mother came to call them to dinner, and she overheard what Jane had said. She was very angry with her, and she petted Lucinda, who allowed herself to be petted. Jane saw Lucinda staring at her with her Pontefract eyes from under Jane's mother's chin.

They sat down to dinner, but Jane's father was not in his place. 'We've run out of orange squash,' said Jane's mother. 'He's just gone to the corner shop to get some.'

'Is it far?' asked Lucinda.

'Just along our street and across the road,' said Jane's mother. 'You can start eating, Lucinda.'

'Does he have to cross a busy road?' asked Lucinda.

'What?' said Jane's mother. 'Oh, yes, busy on a Saturday. But that won't delay him. He's only to wait to cross the road.'

Five minutes later, Lucinda asked if she could have a drink of water, as there still wasn't any orange squash.

Jane's mother got some from the tap, and looked at the clock. 'Where can he have got to?'

'I hope he's all right,' said Lucinda.

'What do you mean, child?'

'I hope he's not been run over,' said Lucinda, looking at Jane as she spoke.

'What rubbish!' said Jane's mother, and sat down suddenly with her hands clasped tightly in her lap.

At that moment, Jane's father walked in with the orange squash. He was surprised that his wife was angry with him for having been so long. He explained that he'd met a friend in the corner shop, and they'd got talking. The friend wanted him to go to a darts match that evening, and he'd said yes.

'Leaving me to babysit?' said Jane's mother.

Jane's father said he hadn't thought of that, but he offered to take Jane and Lucinda to the playground in the Park that afternoon. So it was agreed.

Again, the teddy-bears were left at home. Just before they set out for the Park, Lucinda said she wanted to wear her bobble-hat after all, and ran back into Jane's room to get it. Jane wondered, but her father was holding her fast by the hand, so she couldn't follow Lucinda.

When they came back from the Park, Jane went straight into her bedroom, and – sure enough – there was her teddy with his balaclava on back to front. She put it right. Lucinda, smiling in the doorway, said: 'How naughty of Black Teddy!' Jane glared at her.

That evening, after Jane's father had gone off to his darts match, they watched television. At bedtime, there was Jane's teddy with his balaclava on back to front again, but this time Jane didn't bother to put it right until she was in bed, and her mother was just going to turn out the light. Then she took off the balaclava and the other clothes, and she took her teddy-bear right down under

39

the bedclothes, and whispered: 'Black Teddy is only staying until tomorrow morning. Then he's going home with Lucinda on the coach.' She fell asleep with her teddy-bear in her arms.

She woke because Lucinda was shaking her. Lucinda had drawn back the curtains so that moonlight streamed into the room. She stood by Jane's bed, and in the moonlight her face looked whiter and her eyes looked blacker than by daylight. She was holding Black Teddy right up to the side of her face.

She said softly to Jane: 'Don't make a noise, but listen! Can you hear someone crying?'

'Crying?'

'Sobbing and sobbing. It must be your mother sobbing.'

Jane was frightened. 'I don't think I can hear her. Why should she be sobbing?'

'Because Black Teddy ill-wished your father with his magic eyes.'

'She wouldn't cry because of that,' said Jane firmly. And she was certain now that she couldn't hear anything.

'Ah, but she would cry when she heard what happened to your father on his way home from the darts match after dark.'

'What happened to him?' asked Jane. She hadn't meant to ask; she didn't want to ask; she wouldn't believe what Lucinda was going to say.

Lucinda turned Black Teddy so that he was facing Jane; she brought him forward so that his black eyes were looking into Jane's eyes. 'Listen to what Black Teddy ill-wished,' said Lucinda. 'You remember that corner of the Park where we took a short cut? You remember that slimy pond that your father said was very deep? You remember that thick bush that grows just beside that pond? You remember?'

'Yes,' said Jane faintly.

'Your father decided to take a short cut home in the dark, after the darts match. He was crossing that corner of the Park by the Pond and the bush. It was very dark; it was very lonely. There was someone hiding behind the bush, waiting for your father.'

'Oh, no!'

'He jumped out at your father from behind and hit him on the head, hard, and then he dragged him towards the pond –'

'No, no, no!' With what seemed like one movement Jane was out of bed and in the sitting-room, and there was her mother dozing in front of the television set. She woke up when Jane rushed in, and Jane rushed into her arms. What Jane said was such a muddle and so frantic that her mother thought she had been having nightmares. While she was trying to calm her, Jane's father walked in, very pleased with his darts evening, and perfectly safe and sound.

They tried to understand what Jane tried to tell them. They looked into Jane's bedroom, but there was Lucinda in bed, apparently sound asleep, with Black Teddy clasped in her arms. Even the curtains were drawn close.

They were cross with Jane when she said she wasn't going to sleep in the same room as Lucinda's Black Teddy, but in the end they gave way. They wrapped her in rugs and she slept on the couch in the sitting-room, and Lucinda and Black Teddy had Jane's room to themselves.

'And I don't want to play with her tomorrow morning, and I don't want to see her off at the coach-station, or be with her and her Black Teddy *at all!*' said Jane, when they said a last good-night to her.

On Sunday morning they all had breakfast together, but the little girls spoke not a word to each other. After breakfast Jane's mother said that she would help Lucinda get ready to go home, and Jane's father said he would take Jane to the playground while she was doing that. In the playground, Jane's father often looked at his watch, and they didn't stay there very long. When they got back, Jane's mother and Lucinda had gone. Probably only just gone: Jane's father had timed their return very carefully.

He said: 'Well, that's that! Poor little girl!'

Jane said: 'She was horrible, and she had a horrible Black Teddy.'

'She's very unhappy at home,' said her father. 'We must make allowances. Her mother and father fight like cat and dog. She suffers. That's why your mother asked her for the weekend; but it didn't work.'

'Oh,' said Jane, but she didn't feel sorry for Lucinda at all. She went off to her bedroom – her own bedroom that she wouldn't have to share with Lucinda and Black Teddy any more. And there sat her own dear teddy-bear on her bed, waiting for her. He had his balaclava helmet on back to front, as Lucinda must have arranged it before she left, but that was for the very last time. No more of Black Teddy and his ill-wishing ever again ...

She gazed happily at her teddy-bear, but as she gazed, her happiness seemed to falter, to die in her. She gazed, and thought that her teddy-bear seemed somehow not his usual self. There was something odd about the way he sat, something odd about his paws, something odd about his ears –

She snatched him up and pulled off the balaclava helmet: a pair of black woollen eyes stared at her.

She rushed back to her father, crying: 'She's taken the wrong teddy! Lucinda's stolen my teddy-bear!' She gabbled and wept together.

Her father acted instantly. 'Come on!' he said. 'Bring him with you, and we're off. They've got ten minutes' start of us to the coach-station, but we might be in time. We must catch them before the coach leaves with Lucinda

and Lucinda's suitcase with your teddy in it. Come on –
run!'

They tore out of the house, Jane's father gripping
Jane's hand, and Jane gripping Black Teddy. They ran
and ran: they had to wait at the main road for a gap in
the traffic, and then across, and past the corner shop, and
by the short cut across the Park – there was that dreadful
bush beside that dreadful pond, only it was all bright and
busy this Sunday morning – and on, down another street,
and then another, and Jane was quite breathless, and
there was the coach-station! They went rushing in, and
Jane's father seemed to know where Lucinda's coach
would be, and there it was! There it was, with Jane's
mother talking to the driver, no doubt about putting
Lucinda off at the right place, where she would be
met. And there was Lucinda herself, already sitting
in the coach, with her suitcase in the rack above her
head.

'Stay there!' said her father to Jane, and he took Black
Teddy from her and climbed into the coach. He hadn't
time to say anything to Jane's mother who stared in
amazement, so Jane explained to her mother – and to the
coach driver – while she watched what her father was
doing.

Once he was in the coach, Jane's father stopped being
in a hurry and being excited. He walked to the empty seat
next to Lucinda and sat down in it and spoke to her,
showing her Black Teddy. (Jane could see all this very
clearly through the window of the coach.) He talked to
her, and while he talked he took the trousers and jersey
off Black Teddy and stuffed them into his pocket. Then
he put Black Teddy into Lucinda's arms, but she just let
him fall into her lap. Jane's father went on talking, and
still he didn't take the suitcase from the rack and snatch
Jane's teddy from it, as Jane expected every minute.

At last Jane's father took a handkerchief from his pocket and began dabbing Lucinda's cheeks with it. So Lucinda was crying.

And at last Lucinda stood up on her seat and reached for her suitcase in the rack, and brought it down, and opened it, and took Jane's teddy from it, and gave it to Jane's father. Then he put the suitcase back for her, and tried to put his arm round her and kiss her goodbye, but she wouldn't let him. Then he got off the coach with Jane's teddy-bear.

Jane's father thanked the coach-driver for delaying those few minutes, and he handed Jane her teddy-bear and she hugged him.

Then the coach was off. It moved out of the station towards the great London Road. They were all waving goodbye to Lucinda, even Jane, but she never waved, never looked back.

The coach stopped at the lights before the great road. They couldn't see Lucinda any more, because of the sun's dazzling on the glass of her window. But they could see the window beginning to crawl down: Lucinda must be winding it down from the inside. And Black Teddy appeared at the gap at the top of the window.

The lights changed and the coach moved on again, into the traffic on the great road, gathered speed with the rest of the traffic –

And Black Teddy fell from the window – no, he was *thrown* from the window. Thrown into the middle of the rushing, crushing, cruel traffic.

That was his end.

And the coach went on, out of sight.

Of the three watchers, no one moved; no one spoke. Jane hugged and hugged her own dear teddy to her, and the yellow fur on the top of his head began to be wet with tears. Against her will, she was weeping for what had happened – for all that had happened. She wept for Black Teddy. She wept for Lucinda, too. Now, at last, she felt sorry for Lucinda, and the sorrow was like a pain inside her.

The Road it Went By

We looked down into a deep, dark, oblong hole, my mother and I. Aunt Cass, who stood beside us, said: 'He wanted to be buried in the weedy part of the cemetery. That's what he said: "The weedy part..."'

'It's weedy all right, Aunt Cass,' said my mother.

The gravedigger's spade had shorn through a tangle of greenery into the earth and then through the tangle of roots there. All kinds of roots, from the hair-like roots of grass to the rank, yellow roots that must be nettle, but, among all the others, and more than any other, wriggled pale roots that looked like unpicked white knitting-wool: I recognized Ground Elder. Then the spade had dug deeper still until it reached the barrenness and darkness of the subsoil of my Uncle Percy's grave.

'Yes,' said Aunt Cass, and sighed, and turned away, and we followed. The funeral was not until the next day:

my mother could not attend, and I would not. I had not even wanted to come down with her to see Aunt Cass. But now, suddenly, I felt sorry about Uncle Percy: I had known him so well when I was a small boy, and I remembered the times when he had been kind to me, and gentle.

I had often been sent to stay with my aunt and uncle – they were really my great-aunt and great-uncle, and elderly. They had never had children of their own, and, in their quiet, slow way, they welcomed me. For myself, I was happy to go to them, and to be in a place that was still nearly the country, with big gardens round about where my Uncle Percy worked in his retirement.

Uncle Percy now did jobbing-gardening, and he often took me with him on his jobs.

Mainly, my Uncle Percy dug, and, of course, he weeded as he dug. By far the worst weed in the gardens we visited was Ground Elder (Dog Elder, my uncle called it). And the worst place for Ground Elder was Mrs Hartington's herbaceous border.

Mrs Hartington was rather grand: on no account was her jobbing gardener to come up the front drive to reach the garden, which lay at the back of the house. Instead, he must come by the lane that ran along the bottom of the garden and use the door in the fence there. Mrs Hartington always unlocked the door just before my uncle's arrival.

So Uncle Percy and I entered Mrs Hartington's garden by the door in the fence at the bottom, went past the rubbish heap and the vegetable patch, and so arrived at the lawn and that overgrown border.

Mrs Hartington popped out of the house at once to give her orders to her jobbing gardener: 'Percy, I want you to get on with the digging of the border.'

'Yes, Mrs Hartington, ma'am.'

'And you're always forgetting to light that bonfire. Don't forget again.'

'No, Mrs Hartington, ma'am.'

She went back indoors.

My Uncle Percy began to dig and weed, while I unpacked from my Mickey Mouse suitcase my spacemen and spacewomen and space vehicles and various rubbery monsters. Then I started to build their headquarters and habitations out of stones and twigs and mud. Sometimes I had tried to tell my uncle of the amazing exploits being carried out so close to his feet. Mostly he did not hear me – he was deaf. But, if his hearing-aid was working, he still paid little attention to what he dismissed mildly as my 'rambling on'. The truth is, my uncle had no fancy, no imagination. He was incapable of believing in anything he could not see or hear or touch or smell, or of inventing such a thing. I have always been quite convinced of that.

Besides, later, I had my own experience.

My uncle dug steadily on, weeding as he dug. This was all that was ever expected of him; this was the limit of his gardening skill. He was not clever with plants; really, he was not clever at all, or enterprising. At home, they had only a small back garden, which had been entirely paved over for many years. Aunt Cass grew tomatoes in great pots, but Uncle Percy went there only in summer to take his Sunday nap in a deckchair. He was not exactly a lazy man, but he was slow.

He was also, as I have said, gentle in his speech and in all his ways.

This afternoon I was prattling to him as he dug. Suddenly he said, 'Hush!', and ceased work to bend almost tenderly over the mess of earth and root and stem which he was handling. (This was not the first time he had behaved oddly in Mrs Hartington's garden. Before now I had wondered what my uncle was hearing, or hoped to hear, when he screwed his hearing-aid so firmly into his ear as he weeded. Young as I was, I had decided that he was not really preparing to listen to me or to the birds or perhaps to any ordinary thing in the garden.)

And this was the moment that Mrs Hartington chose to come out on to her garden doorstep, with a mug of tea to be fetched by her jobbing-gardener. (Nothing for me, ever.)

'Percy!' she called.

He was listening to something else. He did not move his head; he did not move at all.

'Percy!' she called again, more sharply.

He ignored her.

She set off across the lawn with an angry briskness, walked straight through my mud-and-twig structures, smashing them, and so reached my uncle. 'Percy!' she said very loudly. 'Your tea!'

Without lifting his head, my uncle said: 'Shut up!'

Mrs Hartington was so startled that she slopped the hot tea from the mug on to the earth of the border. This time he rounded on her and shouted: 'You silly old hen! You'll hurt it!'

My uncle never spoke like that to anyone – let alone to Mrs Hartington. Never.

Mrs Hartington stared at him, dumbstruck with amazement. Only slowly did the words come to her that she judged right.

Meanwhile – '*It?*' I said, and peered at the earth of the border where the tea had splashed. There was nothing to be seen but Ground Elder, rooted or uprooted.

Mrs Hartington had begun speaking: '*Please*,' she said to my uncle – and she sounded the word like a plunging dagger – '*Please*, remember my instructions that a fire should be lit on the rubbish heap at least once a week. You have persistently disobeyed my order in this respect.'

My Uncle Percy did not answer her: he had turned back to his work, and his hearing-aid now dangled free. It seemed insolently to sneer at her.

Mrs Hartington raised her voice: '*Please*, obey my orders. Otherwise the *few* weeds which you have *managed* to dig out of my border will re-invade my garden.'

She wheeled round and went back to the house, still carrying the mug; and my uncle resumed his digging and weeding.

But – *it*?

I stared at the earth, and then peeped at my uncle, a little fearfully. I did not question him, partly because his hearing-aid was still disconnected. In the end, I went back to my play. I had to repair the destruction caused by recent interplanetary attack.

At the end of that afternoon, I walked beside my uncle as he wheeled his barrowload of weeds down to Mrs Hartington's rubbish heap. Then I realized the truth of her complaint: he had not lit a fire there for a long time.

And he was not going to do so now.

He began to empty his fresh load on to the heap. Instead of tipping it all out in one go, he was moving it piecemeal, handful by slow handful. There was something unusual, lingeringly attentive, even loving, in the way he spread his fingers among the roots of the Ground Elder.

I dared to ask him now: 'What is it, Uncle Percy?'

He told me, and I'm sure he told me only because I was just a child: I didn't count. He said: 'There's the root of that Dog Elder, and then there's another thing, like another root, but it's not a root. That other thing winds and twines round the Dog Elder root, like ivy climbing a tree. It uses Dog Elder; Dog Elder root is the road it goes by. It never comes above the earth. I don't know where it comes from, or where it's going, or why, at all. But it sings. No, it doesn't sing, and it doesn't speak. Something else, it does ... I can feel it sometimes ...' He moved his fingers gently among the roots. 'And sometimes I think I can hear it on my whajamacallit ...'

And he screwed his hearing-aid into his ear and bent his head over his recent weedings.

'Can I listen on your hearing-aid, Uncle?'

'No.'

'What's it like? Is it music, then?'

'No, not that either, but it sounds all the time in the earth ...'

After a while he gave a sharp sigh that made me realize that he had been holding his breath. Then he put his handful on to the rubbish heap, and after that he did tip all the rest of the barrowload on to the rubbish-heap. Then he gathered up some good soil from the ground and spread it protectively over the newly dug roots.

Then we were ready to go home.

The next day a brief note arrived from Mrs Hartington for my Uncle Percy. Mrs Hartington would not be requiring my uncle's services again in her garden. She would be making other, more satisfactory, arrangements. His pay to date was enclosed in the envelope.

My Aunt Cass was indignant on my uncle's account, but he did not say much. He started at once on an extraordinary task. He began taking up all the paving stones in their back garden. It was a heavy job for an old man, but he worked steadily at it. Aunt Cass fluttered round him, begging him for reasons and explanations. He gave none.

By the afternoon of the next day, all the paving stones were stacked in one corner of the little garden, exposing an area of bare, sour-looking earth.

'That won't grow anything but weeds,' said my Aunt Cass.

'Yes,' said Uncle Percy.

That evening Uncle Percy went very early to bed. Aunt Cass told me to play quietly, because my uncle was resting. She thought he was resting after his efforts in the back garden; she did not realize that he was resting before further effort.

What happened next was a shock to everyone.

In the very early hours of the morning, the police station received an urgent call from Mrs Hartington. She had heard footsteps on the gravel of her front drive and by the side of the house, and she had glimpsed a figure carrying what she thought was a sack.

The police came at once and, searching Mrs Hartington's garden, found – my Uncle Percy! He would give no explanation of his presence there at that hour. His sack was empty, and there was no clue as to what – if anything – he had intended to put into it. There was no sign of his being about to break into Mrs Hartington's house, in spite of Mrs Hartington's conviction that that had been 'what he was up to'.

In the end, in the face of my uncle's gloomy, unbroken silence, the police decided that the old fellow was a bit off his head. Perhaps the shock of Mrs Hartington's abrupt dismissal had been too much for him. Probably he had had no criminal intention that night – perhaps no clear intention at all. He had always been a bit of an odd old fellow, but at least, in all his life, he had never been anything but law-abiding. Everyone agreed on that. No one in the village had a bad word for Old Perce – except, of course, Mrs Hartington.

The police managed in the end to persuade Mrs Hartington to let the matter drop. At the same time, they suggested to Aunt Cass – who was terribly upset, of course – that she should have a chat with the doctor about Uncle Percy. They also suggested that, in future, she should keep a very sharp watch on him between sunset and sunrise. This she began to do.

In the daytime my Uncle Percy still went jobbing-gardening, although, of course, never at Mrs Hartington's. At first people looked at him a little wonderingly: Mrs Hartington had put her story about, no doubt. But nobody liked Mrs Hartington much, or believed her.

I still went gardening with my uncle, but things were different now. In his slow, silent way, Uncle Percy was unhappy. He dug Ground Elder from other flowerbeds and vegetable plots, but – no, it was not the same. One afternoon, as he finished work, he said to me: 'You're off home tomorrow, boy. Did you know that?'

'Yes, Uncle.'

'Before that, I've something I want you to do.'

'What, Uncle?'

'I'll show you,' he said.

He took me a roundabout way homeward, going by the lane at the bottom of Mrs Hartington's garden. ('She's out,' he said – I don't know how he knew that.) He tried the door in the fence, but, of course, it was locked. The fence was too high for anyone to climb easily, and barbed wire lay along the top. The slats of the fence were set too close for anyone to squeeze through, even a child. But, as we dawdled along the fence, my uncle pulled gently at each slat. All resisted.

Sometimes there was a passer-by in the lane. Whenever anyone appeared, my Uncle Percy was just taking a stroll with his great-nephew. At the end of Mrs Hartington's fence, my uncle turned me round and we walked slowly back along it. Again he tested the slats, pulling a little more strongly this time; and this time he found one that was loose – only very slightly loose – at the bottom. He pulled and shook until the slat was a great deal looser. He brought out a pair of pliers and managed to extract a fastening nail from the bottom of the slat, and another. Now the slat hung only from the top. It looked perfectly in position, like all the other slats, but, in fact, it could be swung to one side or the other to make a narrow gap in the fencing – a narrow entrance into Mrs Hartington's garden.

'You're small enough,' said my uncle. 'You could get through there.'

'But – but –'

'After dark – it would have to be after dark.'

I was appalled.

'You'll easily get through there and get it for me,' he said.

'It?' But I knew what he meant. I began to cry.

He caught me by the shoulders so roughly that it hurt, and he swung me round to face him, and he bent right down to my level. He stared at me with his blue, blue eyes: he stared and stared. I was too frightened to go on crying. He said: 'I must have it.'

'It?'

'I must have it, and you must get it for me. Tonight.' He was whispering, but he might as well have been shouting, yelling, screaming, shrieking. I cowered from the sound of his voice. I had no will of my own against his. Only a child as young as I could get through that narrow gap in the fence, yet I knew I was far too young to be made to undertake such a venture, at night, alone. But I should have to do it.

Late that night, on the excuse to my aunt that he was going to the toilet, Uncle Percy came to my room and roused me. My aunt became aware that more was going on than she knew of.

'What is it?' she called sleepily from their bedroom.

'Little chap's wakeful,' my uncle called back. He helped me quickly to dress. Then I took my Mickey Mouse suitcase, empty, as I had been told. As I crept down the stairs, I heard my uncle getting back into bed beside my aunt.

It wasn't far to the lane at the bottom of Mrs Hartington's garden, and I knew the way, and there was some starlight. But I was terribly frightened, even if I was frightened of nothing. I was a very little boy then, remember. I longed for my mother to be there, or at least for someone safe to meet me and ask: 'What's a little fellow like you doing out all alone in the middle of the night?' But the village street was deserted at such a time.

I reached the lane – the fence – the slat that moved. I swung the slat aside, as I had been shown how, and squeezed myself and my little suitcase through into Mrs Hartington's garden.

The garden was even more frightening than the street and the lane because of the dark, motionless shapes of the bushes and tall plants – or because those shapes looked as if, at any second, they might cease to be motionless. And here, rearing up almost to my own height, was the rubbish heap. I put my suitcase down.

Now I had to follow my uncle's instructions very carefully. I had to face the side of the heap where he had discharged the last load of weeds. I had to thrust my hand into the heap, and count slowly to twenty. If, during that time, I did not feel anything particular, I was to try again in another place. ('What kind of *particular* feeling, Uncle?' 'You'll know, soon enough.')

The first place I tried: nothing. I moved my hand and tried again, noticing how cold my hand was and how it trembled, even inside the earthy heap. Nothing, again. 'I'll try three times and then stop,' I thought. 'Three times, and then I go back.'

How dark it was in the garden – how still – how quiet – By now I was shuddering all over with cold and with

55

fear. I thrust my hand in for the third time, in a third place, and counted up to twenty and more.

Nothing. So now I would go home.

But I was afraid to go back without what my uncle wanted so much. I remembered the violence of his hands on my shoulders; I remembered the glare of his blue eyes.

I thrust my hand into the heap again, and counted; and, before I reached twenty, I began to feel it.

It ...

I did not know whether I felt by touch or whether in some way I heard whatever was there, among the roots of the Ground Elder, clasping, twining, winding, climbing round its roots. Whatever it was, awareness of it flowed into me, for as long as I held my hand there. Was it pain or pleasure that I felt? Whatever it was, I ceased to be frightened, or anxious, or even conscious of what had to be done next. I stood there like a boy enchanted into a statue.

Then some little creature – a field mouse, I think it must have been – ran over my left foot, and roused me.

I closed my hand on what it touched inside the rubbish heap, and I withdrew a handful of roots and earth. I put the handful into my Mickey Mouse case. Then I took another handful and another and another, until the case was full. Then I shut the case and fastened it, and made my way with it back through the fence, along the lane and the village street and in through the front door of my great-uncle's house, which I had left unlatched.

I had been told by my uncle to carry the case through to the garden at the back and leave it there. By the starlight I could just see the raw earth of the garden and, in the middle of it, an oblong blackness – a hole which was just about the size of my Mickey Mouse suitcase. My uncle had told me nothing, but I knew at once that this was a hole he had dug to receive the roots, which were to grow and spread and flourish and fill this little garden.

I left my case by the hole, and went indoors again and upstairs to bed. I knew that Aunt Cass was asleep, by the particular pitch of her snore. I could not hear Uncle Percy's snore. Of course, he could have been sound asleep without snoring, but I did not think so.

I got into bed and put my head under the bedclothes. I gave a gasp, and then I began to cry. I cried and cried. I cried for the fearfulness of that night's lonely, dark journey, and I cried because I had held something in my hand and then had had to let it go. I cried myself to sleep.

The next morning – the morning of my departure – I found my Mickey Mouse suitcase waiting for me downstairs, emptied and clean: I put my space people and my monsters back into it.

There was no oblong hole now to be seen in the middle of the back garden.

That day I went home, and I never came back by myself again. I refused absolutely to go on another visit alone to my Uncle Percy and Aunt Cass, and I refused to explain why I would not go. My mother guessed, I think, that something had frightened me badly, but she could never find out what it was.

So my mother went down by herself, very occasionally, just for the day. She reported that Uncle Percy was becoming odd in his behaviour – odd and oddly happy. He was always digging in the little back garden, she said – digging *with his bare hands*. But never weeding. The garden had become a paradise for weeds, especially Ground Elder. Ground Elder was king there.

When Uncle Percy died at last, my mother persuaded me to go with her to see Aunt Cass. In the end, I was glad I did go. But I've told you all that.

And after it was all over, Mrs Hartington spread a

cruel tale that Aunt Cass had cared so little for her husband that she never planted or even weeded his grave. She may not have weeded it, but I'm sure that she must have planted it – with roots from their own back garden. Uncle Percy would have made her promise to do that. I'm certain of it.

Auntie

Up to the day she died, Auntie could thread the finest needle at one go. She did so on that last rainy day of her life. And, by the end of her life, her long sight had grown longer than anyone could possibly have expected.

Auntie's exceptional eyesight had been of no particular help to her in her job: she was a filing-clerk in a block of offices, for ever sorting other people's dull letters and dull memoranda. Boring; but Auntie was not ambitious, nor was she ever discontented.

Auntie's real interest – all her care – was for her family. She never married; but, by the time of her retirement from work, she was a great-aunt – although she was never called that – and she liked being one. She baby-sat, and took children to school, and helped with family expeditions. She knitted and crocheted and sewed – above all, she sewed. She mended and patched and made clothes.

She sewed by hand when necessary; otherwise she whirred the handle of an ancient sewing-machine that had been a wedding-present to her mother long before.

Unfortunately, she was not particularly good at making clothes. Little Billy, her youngest great-nephew, was her last victim. 'Do I *have* to wear this blazer-thing?' he whispered to his mother, Auntie's niece. (He whispered because – even in his bitterness – he did not want Auntie to overhear.) 'Honestly, Mum, no one at school ever wears anything looking like this.'

'Hush!' said his mother. Then: 'Auntie's very kind to take all that trouble, and to save us money, too. You should be grateful.'

'I'm not!' said little Billy, and he determined that when he was old enough, he wouldn't be at Auntie's mercy any more. Meanwhile, Auntie, who doted on Billy as the last child of his generation, was perplexed by the feeling that something she had done was not quite right.

Auntie was not a thinker, but she had common sense and – more and more – foresight. She knew, for instance, that nobody can live forever. One day she said: 'I wonder when I shall die? And how? Heart, probably. My old dad, your grandad, died of that.'

She was talking to the niece, Billy's mother, with whom Auntie now lived. The niece said: 'Oh, Auntie, don't *talk* so!'

Auntie said: 'My eyesight's as good as ever – well, better, really; but my hands aren't so much use.' She looked at her hands, knobbling with rheumatism. 'I can't use 'em as I once did.'

'Never *mind*!' said the niece.

'And the children are growing up. Even Billy.' Auntie sighed. 'Growing too old for me.'

'The children *love* their auntie!' said the niece angrily. This was true, in its way, but that did not prevent great-nephews and great-nieces becoming irritated when Auntie babied them and fussed over their clothing or over whatever they happened to be doing.

Auntie did not continue the argument with her niece. She was no good at discussion or argument anyway. That wasn't her strong point.

Her eyesight was her strong point, and yet also her worry. In old age she sat for long periods by her bedroom window, looking out over rooftops to distant church spires and tower blocks. 'I don't like seeing so far,' she said once. 'What's the use to me? Or to anyone else?'

'You're lucky,' said her nephew-in-law, Billy's father. 'Some people would give their eyes to – well, they'd give a lot to have your eyesight at your age.'

'It's – it's *wrong*,' said Auntie, trying to explain something.

'If it happens that way, then it's natural,' said her nephew.

'Natural!' said Auntie; and she took to sitting at her bedroom window with her eyes closed.

One day: 'Asleep?' her niece asked softly.

'No.' Auntie's eyes opened at once. 'Just resting my eyes. Trying to get them not to go on with all this looking and looking, seeing and seeing . . .' Here Auntie paused, again attempting to sort out some ideas. But the ideas and what lay behind them could not be as easily sorted and filed into place as those documents in the office where she had worked years ago.

'Ah,' said the niece, preparing to leave it at that.

But Auntie had something more to say. 'When I'm in bed and asleep, I dream, and I know dreams are rubbish, so I needn't pay any attention to them. But when I sit here, wide awake, with my eyes open or even with my eyes closed, then . . .'

The niece waited.

Auntie said carefully: 'Then I think, and thinking must be like seeing: I see things.'

'What things?'

'Things a long way off.'

'That's because you're long-sighted, Auntie.'

'I wouldn't mind that. But the things a long way off are coming nearer.'

'Whatever do you mean?'

'How should I know what I mean? I'm just telling you what *happens*. I see things far away, and they're coming close. I don't understand it. I don't like it.'

'Perhaps you're just having day-dreams, Auntie.'

'You mean, it's all rubbish?'

'Well, is it?'

Auntie moved restlessly in her chair. She hated to be made to think in this way; but there were some things you had to think of with your mind, when you couldn't straightforwardly see them with your eyes and then straightforwardly grasp them with your hands, to deal with them then and there.

There were these other things.

'No,' said Auntie crossly. 'They're not rubbish. All the same, I don't want to think about them. I don't want to talk about them.'

So there was no more talk about the far-away things that were coming nearer; but as for thinking – well, Auntie couldn't help doing that, in her way. Her life was uneventful, so that what she thought about naturally was what she saw with her eyes, or in her mind's eye.

One day the married niece asked if she could use Auntie's old sewing-machine to run up some curtains: her own machine had broken down.

'So has mine,' said Auntie. 'The needle's broken.'

'You have several spare needles, Auntie,' said the niece. 'I think I could put one in.'

The niece went downstairs to where the ancient sewing-machine was kept. When she had unlocked and taken off the wooden lid, she found that the needle was not broken, after all. It did not need replacing. She sighed to herself and smiled to herself at Auntie's mistake; and then she set to work with Auntie's sewing-machine.

She threaded up the machine with the right cotton for her curtains, arranged the material in the right position under the needle, and began to turn the handle of the machine. The stitching began; but the curtain material was very thick, and the needle penetrated it with difficulty ...

With more difficulty at every stitch ...

The needle broke.

So, after all, the niece had to change the needle, to finish machining her curtains. Later on, she said to Auntie: 'Your machine's all right now, but the needle broke.'

'I told you so,' said Auntie.

'No, Auntie. You said the needle *had* broken: you ought to have said, the needle *will* break.' The niece laughed jollily.

'I don't want to say things like that,' said Auntie. She spoke sharply, and her niece saw that she was upset for some reason.

So she said: 'Never mind, Auntie. It was just a funny thing to have happened, after what you said. A coincidence. Think no more of it.'

The niece thought no more of it; but Auntie did. She brooded over the strangeness of her long sight – over the seeing of far-away things that came nearer. She now kept that strangeness private to herself – secret; but sometimes something popped into a conversation before she could prevent it.

One family tea-time, when Auntie had been sitting

silent for some time, she said: 'It's lucky there's never anyone left in those offices at night.'

'Which offices?'

'Where I used to work, of course.'

'Oh . . .' Nobody was interested, except for little Billy. He was always curious. 'Why is it lucky, Auntie?'

But already Auntie regretted having spoken; one could see that. 'No reason . . .' she said. 'Nothing . . . I was just thinking, that's all . . .'

The next morning, with Auntie's early cup of tea, the niece brought news.

'You'll never guess, Auntie!'

'Those old offices are burnt out.'

'Why, you *have* guessed! Yes, it was last night after you'd gone to bed early. An electrical short circuit started the fire, they think. Nobody's fault; and nobody hurt — nobody in the building.'

'No,' said Auntie. 'Nobody at all . . .'

'But you should have seen the blaze! You were asleep, so we didn't wake you; but we took little Billy to see. My goodness, Auntie! The smoke there was!'

'Yes,' said Auntie. 'The smoke . . .'

'And the flames — huge flames towering up!'

'Yes,' said Auntie. 'The whole place quite gutted . . .'

'And all the fire-engines wailing up!'

'Yes,' said Auntie. 'Five fire-engines . . .'

Her niece stared at her: 'There were five fire-engines; but how did you know?'

Auntie was flustered; and the niece went on staring. Auntie said: 'Well, a big blaze like that would *need* five fire-engines, wouldn't it?'

Her niece said nothing more; but, later, she reported the conversation to her husband. He was not impressed: 'Oh, I dare say she woke up and saw the fire through her bedroom window. With her long sight she saw the size of the fire, and – well, she realized it would need at least five fire-engines. As she said, more or less.'

'That's *just* possible as an explanation,' said his wife, 'if it weren't for one thing.'

'What thing?'

'Auntie's bedroom window doesn't look in that direction at all; her old office-block is on the other side of the house.'

'Oh!' said Auntie's nephew-in-law.

In the time that followed, Auntie was very careful indeed not to talk about her sight, long sight, or foresight. Even so, her niece sometimes watched her intently and oddly, as she sat by her bedroom window. And once her nephew-in-law sought her out to ask whether she would like to discuss with him the forthcoming Derby and which horse was likely to win the race. Auntie said she had never been interested in horse-racing, and disapproved of it because of the betting. So that was that.

One afternoon in early spring – not cold, but dreary and very overcast – Auntie was restless. She went downstairs to her sewing-machine and fiddled with it. She did a little hand-sewing on a pair of Billy's trousers, where a seam had come undone. (That was the last time that she threaded a needle.)

Then she went upstairs, and came down again in her coat and hat.

'You're not thinking of going out, Auntie?' cried her niece. 'Today of all days? It's just beginning to rain!'

'A breath of fresh air, all the same,' said Auntie.

'It's not suitable for you, Auntie. So slippery underfoot on the pavements.'

Auntie said: 'I thought I'd go and meet Billy off the school bus.'

'Oh, Auntie! Billy's too old to need meeting off the bus

nowadays. He doesn't need it, and he wouldn't like it. He'd hate it.'

Auntie sighed, hesitated, then slowly climbed up the stairs to her bedroom again.

Five minutes later she was coming downstairs again, almost hurriedly, still hatted and coated. She made for the stand where her umbrella was kept.

'Auntie!' protested the niece.

Auntie patted the handbag she was carrying: 'An important letter I've written, and must get into the post.'

Her niece gaped at her. Auntie never wrote important letters; she never wrote letters at all.

'About my pension,' Auntie explained. 'Private,' she added, as she saw that her niece was about to speak.

Her niece did speak, however. She had quite a lot to say. 'Auntie, your letter *can*'t be all that urgent. And if it is, Billy will be home soon, and he'll pop to the pillar-box for you. It's really ridiculous – *ridiculous* – of you to think of going out in this wet, grey, slippery, miserable weather!'

Suddenly Auntie was different. She was resolved, stern in some strange determination. '*I must go*,' she said, in such a way that her niece shrank back and let her pass.

So Auntie, her umbrella in one hand and her handbag in the other, set out.

The weather had worsened during the short delay. She had to put up her umbrella at once against the rain. She hurried along towards the pillar-box – hurried, but with care, because the pavement and road surfaces were slippery, just as her niece had said.

The pillar-box lay a very little way beyond the bus-stop where Billy's school bus would arrive. There was a constant to and fro of traffic, but no bus was in sight. Instead of going on to the pillar-box, Auntie hesitated a moment, then took shelter from the rain in the doorway of a gent's outfitter's, just by the bus-stop. From inside the shop, an assistant, as he said later, observed the old lady taking shelter, and observed all that happened afterwards.

Auntie let down her umbrella, furled it properly, and held it in her right hand, her handbag in her left.

The shop assistant, staring idly through his shop-window, saw the school bus approaching its stop, through almost blinding rain.

The old lady remained in the doorway.

The school bus stopped. The children began to get off. The traffic swirled by on the splashing road.

The old lady remained in the doorway.

The shop assistant's attention was suddenly caught by something happening out on the road, in the passing traffic. A car had gone out of control on the slippery road. It was swerving violently; it narrowly missed another car, and began skidding across the road, across the back of the school bus. Nearly all the children were away from the bus by now – except for one, slower than the rest. In a moment of horror, the shop assistant saw him, unforgettably: a little boy, wearing a badly made blazer, who was going to be run over and killed.

The assistant gave a cry and ran to the door, although he knew he would be too late.

But someone else was ahead of him, from that same doorway. The old lady darted – no, flung herself – *flew* – forwards towards the child.

There were two – perhaps three – seconds for action before the car would hit the child. The old lady wouldn't reach him in that time; but the assistant saw her swing her right arm forward, the hand clutching a furled umbrella by its ferrule. The crook of the umbrella hooked inside the front of the little boy's blazer and hooked him like a fish from water out of the path of the skidding car.

The old lady fell over backwards on the pavement, with the child on top of her, and the car skidded past them, crashed into the bus-stop itself, and stopped. The driver sat stupefied inside, white-faced, shocked, but otherwise uninjured.

Nobody was injured, except Auntie. She died in the ambulance, on her way to the hospital. Heart, the doctors said. No wonder, at her age, and in such extraordinary circumstances.

Much later, after the funeral, Billy's mother looked for the letter that Auntie had written to the pension people. 'It should have been in her handbag, because the shopman said she didn't go on to the pillar-box to post anything. But it wasn't in her handbag.'

'She must have left it behind by mistake,' said Billy's father. 'She was getting odd in old age. It'll be somewhere in her bedroom.'

'No, I've searched. It isn't there.'

'Why on earth do you want it, anyway?' said Billy's father. 'All that pension business ceases with her death.'

'I don't want the letter,' said his wife. 'I just want to know whether there ever was one.'

'What are you driving at?'

'Don't you see? The letter was an excuse.'

'An excuse?'

'She wanted an excuse to be at that bus-stop when Billy got off, because she knew what was going to happen. She foresaw.'

They stared at each other. Then the nephew said: 'Second sight – that's what you mean, isn't it? But it's one thing to foresee, say, which horse is going to win the Derby. And it's quite another thing to foresee what's going to happen, and then deliberately to prevent its happening. That's altering the course of things . . . That's altering everything . . .'

The niece said: 'But you don't understand. She foresaw that Billy would be in danger of being killed, so she went to save him. But she also foresaw that very thing – I mean, she foresaw that she would go to save him. That she *would* save him. Although it killed her.'

The nephew liked a logical argument, even about illogical things. He said: 'She could still have altered that last part of what she foresaw. She could have decided *not* to go to the bus-stop, because she foresaw that it would all end in her death. After all, nobody wants to die.'

'You still don't understand,' his wife said. 'You don't understand Auntie. She knew she would save Billy, even if she had to die for it. She had to do it, because it was her nature to do it. Because she was Auntie. Don't you *see*?'

The nephew, seeing something about Auntie he had never properly perceived before, said quite humbly: 'Yes, I see . . .'

And the niece, leaning on his shoulder, wept again for Auntie, whom she had known so well since she had been a very little girl. Known so well, perhaps, that she had not known Auntie truly for what she really was, until then.

As for Billy, he never said much about that rainy day, the last of Auntie's life. He hadn't gone to Auntie's funeral – children often don't. But he wore his horrible, home-made blazer until he grew out of it. And he never, never forgot Auntie.

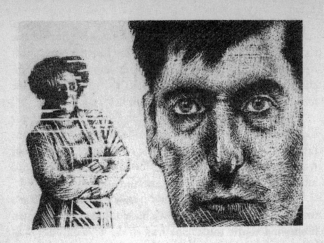

His Loving Sister

When I was a child, my best friend lived next door. He was Steve Phillips, and he had an elder brother and a little sister. After they were all killed, my mother used to hug me and say: 'There but for the grace of God . . .' Meaning that I might have been killed, too.

My mother had known Mrs Phillips – Lizzie Phillips – all her life. Ours was that sort of village in those days. Our family got on very well with all the Phillips family – except for one thing. My parents didn't like Lizzie Phillips's brother, Billy Peterman, who ran the only garage in the village and lived over it. He was much younger than his sister; and he was the kind of man who always would look young: rosy cheeks, and innocent blue eyes, and fair, tousled hair.

In fact, my father couldn't bear Billy Peterman.

My father used to get angry about quite a lot of things,

and he said that most garages were crooked somewhere, but the Daffodil Garage was run by a crook. My mother said that Billy Peterman wasn't really a crook; just weak and lazy. He always had been, even as a little boy. Then my father asked her, where had Billy Peterman got the money to run a garage, anyway, unless he'd sponged off his sister and her family? My mother didn't answer that, but she would wind up the argument by saying that Lizzie Phillips really loved Billy. She had brought him – and their sister – up, when their mother had died. The sister had married young and gone to Canada. That left just Lizzie and Billy. When Lizzie married and had children, she still loved Billy and cared for him as if he were another, older child; and Billy let her.

My father snorted. The only dealings with the Daffodil Garage that my father would allow himself were for petrol and oil. He always checked his change carefully afterwards.

We knew the Phillipses so well that every morning in term-time Mr Phillips drove me with his own children to school in Ponton. He worked in Ponton, and he dropped us off at school on the way. I used to sit with Steve and Lily on the back seat of the car; and Peter, the eldest of their three children, sat at the front with his father.

Of course, the Phillipses had to use the Daffodil Garage, because of the family connection. Mr Phillips never talked much, anyway, and he didn't grumble; but my father said he must often have been fed up. Sometimes their car had to go back over and over again for the same thing to be put right. And once – and this is where the story really starts – the repairs dragged on for so long that Billy Peterman had to lend another car – one of his own – to the family. On the very day that happened, I started with whooping-cough.

I was in bed upstairs, and my mother was downstairs.

My mother could always be at home in the mornings. She worked afternoons, and Lizzie worked mornings, in the same shop in the village. You can see what a useful arrangement that was when we were little: always one mother at home if anything went wrong in either family.

Well, Mrs Phillips had gone off to work and all the rest of the Phillipses had gone off to Ponton in the car from the Daffodil Garage. My father had gone to work, and there was just my mother and me.

It was quiet and very peaceful. My coughing had tired me, so I was glad just to lie back on the pillows. My mother had drawn my bed forward so that I could see out of the window and into the street outside. She thought I might be interested to watch the passers-by. But there hadn't really been any that morning.

But now a police car came cruising slowly down the street. To my amazement, it stopped quite near our house. A policewoman got out and went up the path to the Phillipses front door, and rang the bell. There was no answer, of course.

After a while the policewoman came down the path again and into the road, and had a word with the police-driver. Then she stood and looked thoughtfully at the Phillipses' house and at the houses on either side. You could almost see her wondering which of the two neighbours to try next.

She decided on our house. She opened the front gate and walked up the path. Then I lost sight of her under the front porch, but I heard the bell ring, and my mother stopped hoovering and went to answer it.

It all seemed very odd to me, because the policewoman came right into the house at once, and my mother took her into the sitting-room and shut the door. By this time, in spite of the whooping-cough, I was out of bed and at the bedroom door, listening. All I could hear were two voices – mostly the policewoman's – talking in low tones. It was quite a while before my mother showed the policewoman out. She went back to her police car and was driven away.

I nipped back into bed, and called to my mother to come and tell me about whatever it was. She didn't answer. There was a long, long silence from downstairs. I didn't know why, but I was frightened . . .

Then I heard my mother's feet coming slowly up the stairs. She came into my bedroom. I had never, never seen her looking like that before. Her face was quite white, with staring eyes, from which rolled down tears and tears and tears.

She wasn't seeing me at all; and then suddenly she was. She made a strange, huge leap across the room to me, almost like a kangaroo, and she clutched me in her arms and hugged me there until I could hardly breathe. That was when she first said: 'There but for the grace of God . . .'

Yes, all three children had been killed outright, and their father.

They had been driving down the hill from our village to join the main road to Ponton at the T-junction. Ours was a minor road; the Ponton road was a major one. So the Ponton traffic on it had the right of way; and when I had been with them, Mr Phillips often had to wait at the T-junction. He was a careful, good driver.

That morning, one of those huge container-lorries was going along the main road at a moderate pace, and coming up to the T-junction. The driver saw the Phillipses' car approaching from a distance. He expected to see it beginning to slow up to stop; but he saw it was still coming on quite fast. He still expected it to stop; and then, the lorry-driver said, he caught a glimpse through the windscreen of the other driver's face – Mr Phillips's face. Even at the distance that still separated them, he saw the horror on it. *The car couldn't stop.* The lorry-driver put on his brakes and swerved, but too late. The car from the Daffodil Garage crashed into the side of the lorry, and everyone in it was killed.

The lorry-driver was all right, but terribly shaken. The accident hadn't been his fault at all, of course. But whose fault was it then? 'I tell you, I saw his face,' the lorry-driver kept saying. 'He *couldn't* stop. I saw his face ...'

What was left of the car was towed to the nearest garage, which was the Daffodil. In due course the police examined it carefully, but found nothing wrong.

My father, at home, exploded. 'Nothing wrong! Of course there was nothing wrong by the time that crook Billy Peterman had seen to it. But the brakes must have failed, mustn't they? He ought never to have let that car out of his garage with brakes in that condition. He killed the four of them, and then – to save his own skin – he tinkered and put things right, before the police got on to him!'

'Hush!' said my mother. 'Hush, hush, hush! Don't say such things, even if they're true. Suppose Lizzie ever heard you?'

'Heard me?' cried my father. 'Don't you think she *knows* her brother killed them?'

As I look back now, that time of my childhood seems to have been dark and muddled and strange. Suddenly I hadn't a best friend any more. My father was angry for a lot of the time. My mother cried a lot of the time; and she slept at nights in the Phillipses' house, so that Lizzie Phillips should not be quite alone.

I suppose there was a funeral, or four funerals. Lizzie Phillips's sister flew over from Canada. She stayed with Lizzie, and she was very brisk and businesslike. She told us that Lizzie had agreed to go back to Canada with her, and settle there.

'Will she like that?' my mother asked doubtfully.

'There's nothing for her *here*,' said the brisk Canadian.

'There's nothing for her anywhere,' said my mother sadly.

We saw Lizzie go. Her face was a strange pale colour; her eyes were dead. She kissed my mother goodbye; but my mother said afterwards that she had felt as if she were kissing a statue of somebody. Lizzie drove away with her sister.

'I wonder if she'll be able to stick it out there,' said my father. 'I think she'll come back.'

'No,' said my mother. 'I don't think she cares enough about anything now. I don't think she will.'

But, as it turned out later, my father was the one who was right.

What about Billy Peterman all this time? Of course, we didn't know all the ins and outs of the family's affairs; but we knew that Lizzie had absolutely refused to see him after the accident. She left for Canada without having said goodbye to him.

Billy Peterman went on running his Daffodil Garage, apparently just as usual.

For a long time, I was remembering – when I least wanted to – two faces: my mother's face on that whooping-cough morning, running over with tears; and Lizzie Phillips's face when she came to say goodbye, like carved stone. And I missed Steve terribly. One afternoon, without telling anybody, I walked all the way from our village down the hill to the T-junction with the main road to Ponton. I stood there, just looking, for a long time. Dusk was beginning to fall, and there were already lights on the cars and lorries as they came and went along the main road. I wished Steve weren't dead. I wished he were alive to play with me again. Suddenly I was frightened that I would call him back.

He would come: his ghost . . .

I turned tail and fled up the hill again. I never went back alone on foot to that T-junction again.

Meanwhile, as people do, we began to live ordinary lives once more. Another family moved into the house next door, and we got on well with them, although not quite as well as with the Phillipses. I played with the children sometimes.

I think now that my mother must have missed Lizzie's friendship very much indeed. After all, they had known each other since they were little girls together. She wrote several times to Canada, but there was no reply.

My father recovered more easily. He still had a hate against the Daffodil Garage, but occasionally he would drop in for petrol, if his tank were empty. After such a call, he came home to us quite excited: 'I told you so! Lizzie Phillips is back! She couldn't stand Canada and that bossy sister.'

'Where is she?' cried my mother. 'Where's she staying? Why hasn't she come to us?'

'I suppose she's staying with Billy – I saw her in Billy's office at the garage, standing by his cash desk. She wasn't actually talking to him, but there she was.'

My mother was startled. 'She couldn't be staying with him!' she said. 'Not after what he did! Never!' (That was really the only time my mother let slip that she thought my father was right about Billy Peterman's responsibility for the accident.)

'Well, you always used to say she was a loving sister,' said my father. 'Anyway, wherever she's staying, she's sure to be round here soon to see you.'

But Lizzie Phillips didn't call.

My mother waited a day; she waited two. She felt hurt

that such an old friend as Lizzie should be in the same village and not come to see her. In the end, she decided to go herself and call on Lizzie at the Daffodil Garage – if that were really where she was staying. She took me with her. I think she was nervous, and wanted the company even of a child.

As we walked into the forecourt of the garage, my mother said: 'Surely – yes, there she is!' I thought I saw the figure of a woman slipping away out of sight. My mother called: 'Lizzie! Lizzie! Please!'

But no one came forward to her.

My mother went on to where Billy Peterman was sitting in his little office – just sitting. He was a lazy young man, as my mother always said; but he didn't exactly look as if he were lazing comfortably at his desk now. He would always look a young man, but now he suddenly looked an old young man. The roses in his cheeks had faded, his fair hair looked dull and dusty, his blue eyes gazed vacantly at my mother. He had seen her coming – he must have done; and he must have heard her calling. But he made no move.

My mother went quite close to him. 'Lizzie's here now, isn't she?'

'Yes,' he said.

'I want to see her,' my mother said.

'Well,' he said, in a flat voice, 'you have seen her, haven't you? She's always here now. With me.'

'I want to see her and talk to her,' my mother insisted.

He shook his head.

'What do you mean, Billy Peterman? You can't keep her to yourself!'

He laughed in a strange, flat way. Then he said: 'Lizzie died in Canada ten days ago. The letter said she didn't want to live any longer. They said she died of a broken heart.'

My mother stared and stared at him. She had never really liked Billy Peterman; none of us did. But she had known him as a little boy, and she was easily touched to pity. Now she said, as if she really meant it: 'Poor, poor Billy . . .'

He turned his head aside, so that we should not see his face.

Very soon after that, Billy Peterman sold the Daffodil Garage and moved away. No one knew where he went, or ever heard of him again.

What I have often wondered since is this: Did his loving sister go with him?

Who's Afraid?

'Will my cousin Dicky be there?'

'Everyone's been asked. Cousins, aunts, uncles, great-aunts, great-uncles – the lot. I've told you: it's your great-grandmother's hundredth birthday party.'

'But will Dicky Hutt be there?'

'I'm sure he will be.'

'Anyway, Joe, why do you want to know?'

Joe's mother and father were staring at Joe; and Joe said, 'I hate Dicky.'

'Now, Joe!' said his mother; and his father asked: 'Why on earth do you hate Dicky?'

'I just do,' said Joe. He turned away, to end the conversation; but inside his head he was saying: 'I'd like to kill Dicky Hutt. Before he tries to kill me.'

When the day of the birthday came, everyone – just as

Joe's mother had said – was there. Relations of all ages swarmed over the little house where Great-grandmother lived, looked after by Great-aunt Madge. Fortunately, Great-grandmother had been born in the summer, and now – a hundred years later – the sun shone warmly on her celebrations. Great-aunt Madge shooed everyone into the garden for the photograph. The grown-ups sat on chairs, or stood in rows, and the children sat cross-legged in a row in the very front. (At one end, Joe; at the other, Dicky; and Dicky's stare at Joe said: 'If I catch you, I'll kill you . . .') There was a gap in the centre of this front row for a table with the tiered birthday cake and its hundred candles.

And behind the cake sat Great-grandmother in her wheelchair, with one shawl over her knees and another round her shoulders. Great-aunt Madge stood just behind her.

Great-grandmother faced the camera with a steady gaze from eyes that saw nothing by now – she had become blind in old age. Whether she heard much was doubtful. Certainly, she never spoke or turned her head even a fraction as if to listen.

After the photograph and the cutting of the cake, the grown-ups stood around drinking tea and talking. (Great-grandmother had been wheeled off somewhere indoors for a rest.) The children, if they were very young, clung to their parents; the older ones sidled about aimlessly – aimlessly, except that Joe could see Dicky always sidling towards him, staring his hatred. So Joe sidled away and sidled away . . .

'Children!' cried Great-aunt Madge. 'What about a good old game? What about hide-and-seek? There's the garden to hide in, and most of the house.'

Some of the children still clung to their parents; others said 'yes' to hide-and-seek. Dicky Hutt said 'yes'. Joe said 'no'; but his father said impatiently: 'Don't be soft! Go off and play with the others.'

Dicky Hutt shouted: 'I'll be He!' So he was. Dicky Hutt shut his eyes and began to count at once. When he had counted a hundred, he would open his eyes and begin to search.

Joe knew whom he would search for with the bitterest thoroughness: himself.

Joe was afraid – too afraid to think well. He thought at first that he would hide in the garden, where there were at least grown-ups about – but then he didn't trust Dicky not to be secretly watching under his eyelashes, to see exactly where he went. Joe couldn't bear the thought of that.

So, after all, he went indoors to hide; but by then some of the best hiding-places had been taken. And out in the garden Dicky Hutt was counting fast, shouting aloud his total at every count of ten. 'Seventy!' he was shouting now; and Joe had just looked behind the sofa in the front room, and there was already someone crouching there. And there was also someone hiding under the pile of visitors' coats – 'Eighty!' came Dicky Hutt's voice from the garden – and two children already in the stair-cupboard, when he thought of that hiding-place. So he must go on looking for somewhere – anywhere – to hide – and 'Ninety!' from outside – *anywhere* to hide – and for the second time he came to the door with the notice pinned to it that said: 'Keep out! Signed: Madge.'

'A hundred! I'm coming!' shouted Dicky Hutt. And Joe turned the handle of the forbidden door and slipped inside and shut the door behind him.

The room was very dim, because the curtains had been drawn close; and its quietness seemed empty. But Joe's eyes began to be able to pick out the furnishings of the room, even in the half-light: table, chair, roll-top desk, and also – like just another piece of furniture, and just as immobile – Great-grandmother's wheelchair and Great-grandmother sitting in it.

He stood, she sat, both silent, still; and Dicky Hutt's thundering footsteps and voice were outside, passing the door, and then far away.

He thought she did not know that he had come into her room; but a low, slow voice reached him: 'Who's there?'

He whispered: 'It's only me – Joe.'

Silence; and then the low, slow voice again: 'Who's there?'

He was moving towards her, to speak in her very ear, when she spoke a third time: 'Who's there?'

And this time he heard in her voice the little tremble of fear: he recognized it. He came to her chair, and laid his hand on hers. For a second he felt her weakly pull away, and then she let his hand rest, but turned her own, so that his hand fell into hers. She held his hand, fingered it slowly. He wanted her to know that he meant her no harm; he wanted her to say: 'This is a small hand, a child's hand. You are only a child, after all.'

But she did not speak again.

He stood there; she sat there; and the excited screams and laughter and running footsteps of hide-and-seek were very far away.

At last, Joe could tell from the sounds outside that the game of hide-and-seek was nearly over. He must be the last player not to be found and chased by Dicky Hutt. For now Dicky Hutt was wandering about, calling: 'Come out, Joe! I know where you're hiding, Joe, so you might as well come out! I shall find you, Joe – I shall find you!'

The roving footsteps passed the forbidden doorway several times; but – no, this time they did not pass. Dicky Hutt had stopped outside.

The silence outside the door made Joe tremble: he tried to stop trembling, for the sake of the hand that held his, but he could not. He felt that old, old skin-and-bony hand close on his, as if questioning what was happening, what was wrong.

But he had no voice to explain to her. He had no voice at all.

His eyes were on the knob of the door. Even through the gloom he could see that it was turning. Then the door was creeping open – not fast, but steadily; not far, but far enough –

It opened far enough for Dicky Hutt to slip through. He stood there, inside the dim room. Joe could see his bulk there: Dicky Hutt had always been bigger than he was; now he loomed huge. And he was staring directly at Joe.

Joe's whole body was shaking. He felt as if he were shaking to pieces. He wished that he could.

His great-grandmother held his shaking hand in hers.

Dicky Hutt took a step forward into the room.

Joe had no hope. He felt his great-grandmother lean forward a little in her chair, tautening her grip on his hand as she did so. In her low, slow voice she was saying: 'Who –' And Joe thought, He won't bother to answer her; he'll just come for me. He'll *come* for me . . .

But the low, slow voice went on: 'Whoooooooooooooooooo –' She was hooting like some ghost-throated owl; and then the hooting raised itself into a thin, eerie wailing. Next, through the wailing, she began to gibber, with effect so startling – so horrifying – that Joe forgot Dicky Hutt for a moment, and turned to look at her. His great-grandmother's mouth was partly open, and she was making her false teeth do a kind of devil's dance inside it.

And when Joe looked towards Dicky Hutt again, he

had gone. The door was closing, the knob turning. The door clicked shut, and Joe could hear Dicky Hutt's feet tiptoeing away.

When Joe looked at his great-grandmother again, she was sitting back in her chair. Her mouth was closed; the gibbering and the hooting and the wailing had ceased. She looked exhausted – or had she died? But no, she was just looking unbelievably old.

He did not disturb her. He stood by her chair some time longer. Then he heard his parents calling over the house for him: they wanted to go home.

He moved his hand out of hers – the grasp was slack now: perhaps she had fallen asleep. He thought he wanted to kiss her goodbye; but then he did not want the feel of that century-old cheek against his lips.

So he simply slipped away from her and out of the room.

He never saw her again. Nearly a year later, at home, the news came of her death. Joe's mother said: 'Poor old thing . . .'

Joe's father (whose grandmother Great-grandmother had been) said: 'When I was a little boy, she was fun. I remember her. Joky, then; full of tricks . . .'

Joe's mother said: 'Well, she'd outlived all that. Out-lived everything. Too old to be any use to herself – or to anyone else. A burden, only.'

Joe said nothing; but he wished now that he had kissed her cheek, to say goodbye, and to thank her.

Mr Hurrel's Tallboy

I was only a child at the time, so – just to please me, I suppose – I had been given the job of listening for the knocks on the party-wall. (My bedroom-playroom was right against the wall that divided us from our next door neighbours, the Hurrels. And, in fact, I could hear much more than deliberate knocking through that thin wall. But all that comes later.)

The knocking came: a cheerful *rat-tat-tat*!

I rushed downstairs, where my mother and father were already waiting. We trooped through our front door and down our front path, through our front gate, sharp right for a step or two, and then sharp right again through the Hurrels' gate and up their path to their front door.

The door stood open, with Mrs Hurrel – tiny, frail, gasping with excitement – welcoming us in. The ground floor of their house was Mr Hurrel's workshop, with all his tools and timber – he was a retired furniture restorer and cabinet-maker. We were taken upstairs to their living-room, which was the room next to mine, with the party-wall in between.

Against this wall stood the tallboy.

I was prepared – I had been prepared by my parents' explanations – for the appearance of the tallboy. I knew that it was so very tall only because it was really two chests of drawers, made to fit with beautiful exactitude one on top of the other: the lower section had three long drawers, and stood on four elegant little splayed-out legs. The upper section had three long drawers and, at the very top, a pair of short ones.

All that was no surprise to me. What I was not prepared for was the awe-inspiring magnificence – the *majesty* – of the tallboy. Its surface of polished wood glowed richly; its head reared almost to the ceiling. It dwarfed into insignificance the figure of Mr Hurrel, who stood beside it. Yet he had made it; it was his. It was as if, all those years, ordinary-looking, ordinary-sized Mr Hurrel had had this tallboy inside him, imprisoned, cramped, struggling to get out. Now it was out; and it stood there in its full splendour: a masterpiece of furniture.

The tallboy was Mr Hurrel's masterpiece; it was also his whim. Nobody, really, made tallboys nowadays – hadn't done so, seriously, for well over a hundred years. But, in his job, Mr Hurrel had had to repair antique tallboys; and the dazzling idea had come to him of making one of his own. He had worked on it in his spare time for several years, and now, in retirement, he had finished it at last.

Mr Hurrel stood by his tallboy, smiling only a little. He said nothing, because he had nothing to say. His tallboy spoke for him.

My mother was exclaiming at the number of drawers: 'The storage space!'

The Hurrels' grown-up son, Denis, who had taken time off from his job in Scotland for the occasion, said: 'Mum has to stand on a chair to reach the top drawers!'

'Yes, just fancy!' said Mrs Hurrel breathlessly. Her son put an arm affectionately round her shoulder, and laughed.

The only other person in the room was the Hurrels' daughter, Wendy. She was much older than her brother, unmarried, and working in London. She came home sometimes, but we never felt that we knew her well. She was pale, insignificant-looking, silent.

Mrs Hurrel was pulling out one of the drawers of the tallboy to show my mother the quantity of sheets, tablecloths and other things she was able to keep there. The drawer pulled out smoothly – smoothly; and, when it was pushed back, there was a tiny puff of air – a sigh of air escaping at the last moment (I had very sharp ears, in those days; I heard it), so perfect was the fit.

My father was respectfully questioning Mr Hurrel about the making of the tallboy; and Mr Hurrel, after all, was taking pleasure in answering him – you could see that. He spoke of mortise-and-tenon and dowel-pegging and the dovetailing – the finest – of the fronts and backs of all the drawers; of canted front corners and dentil-moulding and cross-grained banding and cock-beading. He spoke of the woods he had used: pine for the back and for the cornice-framing; oak for the drawers; but everywhere else, solid mahogany or mahogany veneer. 'Honduras mahogany,' said old Mr Hurrel. 'Only the best . . .'

I was gazing at the wooden handles of the drawers: from the centre of each knob a little star twinkled at me. 'Are they really gold?' I asked, because the tallboy deserved only the best.

Mr Hurrel did not laugh at me. 'Not gold,' he said. 'Brass. I've always fancied that decoration. And wooden handles for the drawers – they were my fancy, too.'

While we were talking, Denis had brought a bottle of champagne out of the fridge, and his mother had brought glasses. My father said jovially that someone ought to smash the bottle against the side of the tallboy, to launch it, as they used to do with ocean-going liners. Mr Hurrel shuddered, and his wife said quickly: 'Nobody's ever going to hurt your tallboy, Edward.' And, indeed, when Denis opened the champagne bottle, he was careful to turn away from the tallboy, so that the cork flew out in the opposite direction.

Then we all drank our glasses of champagne, toasting the new tallboy, and Mr Hurrel, its maker, and Mrs Hurrel, his wife. We wished them health and long life. It was the first time I had ever tasted champagne. It seemed to explode in my mouth in rockets of liquid excitement. To my mind the champagne and the tallboy went together: both dizzyingly splendid. Sublime.

But our champagne-wishes did not, alas, come true.

Mrs Hurrel had always been delicate, and, not long after our celebrations, she had to take to her bed. There was even talk of her going into hospital, but she wouldn't have that. So old Mr Hurrel nursed her, and did the housekeeping as best he could. And the arrangement was that he would knock on the party-wall if he needed help urgently. Twice he did that, and woke me, and I woke my mother, and she went round, even in the middle of the night.

Wendy came for a weekend, and helped; and Denis came for another weekend. He suggested taking his mother back to Scotland with him – and his father, too, of course: he had a house in Scotland and was marrying a Scottish girl, so there would be a home for them. The old people wouldn't hear of it.

Denis Hurrel came round to talk to my parents. You could see that he was worried. He'd been talking to Wendy on the telephone: he thought she would come down to help again.

'Just for the weekend?'

'No.' He looked uncomfortable. 'I didn't suggest anything to her, I promise you; and, anyway, it's not ideal. But she's likely to come for good.'

My parents were startled, and very doubtful. 'Give up her job? Leave all her friends in London?'

'She hasn't any friends,' Denis said quickly. 'So she says. And she's always had this idea she'd like to queen it at home – be housekeeper for my dad. She never really got on with Mum for that very reason, I think. She wanted Dad to herself, always.'

'But, Denis, it's your mother she'll have to care for. Constant attention.'

'Wendy'll manage that; and, in return, she'll have the running of the house for Dad.'

'Well, I don't know, I'm sure . . .' my mother said.

'Look! If you get worried, ring me in Scotland. I'll come.'

'There!' said my father. 'That sounds all right to me.'

And so it was, for a long time. Wendy did the shopping and the cooking and house-cleaning, and nursed her mother. Old Mrs Hurrel became a permanent invalid, but she was fairly cheerful. How long she would live was another matter, people said.

Mr Hurrel never seemed to notice Wendy and all that she was doing for him. She might not have been there, for the attention he paid to her. He cared only for his furniture – his tallboy particularly. He was always polishing it. It was his darling, his magnificent child.

And Wendy? Nobody knew what she thought of life with her parents.

And then one day, suddenly, one of those parents died. No, not invalid Mrs Hurrel, but Mr Hurrel. He died in his sleep – heart disease, according to the doctor. His wife was terribly upset, of course; and so was Denis, when he came for the funeral. Again, he tried to persuade his mother to move up to Scotland: she refused. 'I stay here,' she said, 'where he made his beautiful tallboy. Wendy will look after me.'

As for Wendy herself, if she had been rather taciturn before, she was almost speechless now. You felt that the death of her father had embittered her. I was frightened of her because I had this feeling that now she was bottling something up inside her. Something larger than herself. And dark. And very frightening.

'I don't think Denis should have left Wendy in sole charge of the old lady,' my mother said uneasily. 'I've a good mind to ring Scotland and tell him so.' But she didn't.

At first there seemed nothing particular to worry about, except that Mrs Hurrel told us that Wendy no longer spoke to her at all. Nor did she acknowledge our greetings in the street. Nor did she greet us with even a word whenever we rang at the Hurrels' front door.

'Cooped up in that house for most of the time, not talking,' said my mother. 'It's not natural. She'll begin to go off her head.'

My father said: 'She'll begin talking to the furniture.'

'She does,' I said, pleased to add an item of solid fact to the conversation. 'I can hear her through the wall. She bangs about a lot, and she talks to the furniture.'

They stared at me. '*Talks to the furniture?*'

I didn't realize until then that my father had only been joking: no one is supposed literally to talk to furniture.

'Or perhaps she talks just to the tallboy,' I suggested, trying in some way to make the whole thing sound more likely.

They came to my room that evening, put their ears to the party-wall, and listened. You couldn't distinguish the words, but you could recognize the voice: it was Wendy all right. Her tone was bitter and furiously accusing; and, as well as talking, she was violently banging about, as I had said.

My father whispered: 'She really is going off her head.'

My mother whispered back: 'She shouldn't be looking after that poor old dear, helpless in bed.'

They went downstairs at once, to telephone to Scotland.

If they had not gone off so promptly, I should have asked them to wait, and to go on listening, with more care still. In the pauses in Wendy's raving and banging, there was something else one could just hear: a sound that was not exactly a voice, and yet, goaded, it spoke, as it seemed: it *replied*.

On the telephone Denis Hurrel promised my mother to come home that very weekend.

That Friday evening my mother gave my father his tea, and then went out to call on a friend. I was upstairs. I felt easier in my room than usual, because there was no sound from the other side of the party-wall. Wendy was elsewhere in the Hurrels' house, or perhaps out of the house altogether – but that was very seldom nowadays.

Our front door bell rang. I paid no attention to the caller: my dad was there to deal with whoever it was.

Later, my mother came back; and, soon after, I came downstairs to be with them. Wendy had started up again, on the other side of the party-wall, worse than ever before.

Downstairs, my father was telling my mother about the visitor. 'I was taken aback. I mean, Wendy's never called round before.'

'Was it about her mother?'

'No, and I didn't have time to ask about her. Wendy was in such a hurry – such a state – to borrow our axe.'

'To borrow *what*?'

'Our axe – our hatchet.' My father's voice faltered as he saw my mother's expression. 'It's all right. Really. She only wanted it to chop wood for their fire.'

My mother said: 'The Hurrels haven't an open fire anywhere in that house.' My father's jaw dropped. My mother was crying: 'Oh, that poor old thing in bed! Oh, my God! And you lent her an axe!'

My mother had started for the front door, but my father passed her. I followed them out of the house: I was too frightened to be left behind, alone.

We ran down to our front gate, in through the Hurrels' and up to their front door. As we came up the path, we could see the light in Mrs Hurrel's bedroom, upstairs, and we could hear Wendy's voice, raised high.

My father rang the doorbell and, at the same time, lifted the flap of the letter-box, to call through it. He never did so, because the lifting of the flap allowed us to hear more clearly what was going on upstairs. Wendy was now shouting at the top of her voice: 'I'll kill you!' she howled. 'I'll kill you!'

No one had ever thought of my father as a particularly strong man – I do not think he thought that of himself. But instantly he had drawn back and then run at the door like a battering-ram – and we flung ourselves upon the door at the same time. The door-fastenings broke, and we all fell inside.

At the same time, from above, came a woman's scream, with a great crash. My father and mother tore upstairs to Mrs Hurrel's bedroom. I hid under the stairs, too terrified to follow them, this time. So I know only what they chose to tell me, later.

They found old Mrs Hurrel sitting on the edge of her bed, white-faced and shivering, trying to stand up, trying to walk. She kept saying that she must go to Wendy; Wendy was in the living-room; something terrible had happened to Wendy.

They went into the living-room.

Wendy lay on the floor, dead – a glance was enough to confirm that – with the tallboy on top of her. She still held in her grip the axe – our axe. She had evidently been attacking the tallboy with the axe, particularly chopping at its legs. In her fury, she did not foresee the consequences – or perhaps she did not care. She had severed one front leg completely; the other one was splintered, and had broken. The tallboy had tottered and the upper section had fallen forwards, all its drawers shooting out ahead of it in their smooth, their deadly, way. She had not sprung back in time to escape, and the upper drawers had caught her about the head and face and neck, and the fall of the upper casing upon her had completed the tallboy's counter-assault, or self-defence. The contents of the drawers lay in confusion all about the body, white cotton and linen stained with Wendy's blood.

All this I learnt only bit by bit, and much later: I was a child, to be shielded from nightmares. I was sent to stay for some time with a school-friend living the other side of town. When I was finally allowed home, a great deal had happened in my absence: the inquest, and the funeral, for instance. Old Mrs Hurrel was to live with Denis and his new wife in Scotland; and meanwhile he was clearing the house and putting it up for sale.

'What about the – ?' My father could not get the word out.

My mother said: 'What about the tallboy, Denis? Your father could have repaired it, if he were still alive. Perhaps another craftsman as clever as he was ...'

'No,' said Denis. 'No.' He looked strangely at them, and then told some story about a dog that, at first, seemed to me to have nothing to do with the tallboy and its ruination. He said the dog, a big, beautiful creature, a pedigree, belonged to a master with a vicious streak in him. The man tormented and beat the dog cruelly; and one day the dog turned on the man and savaged him, so that the man died.

'It wasn't really the dog's fault,' said Denis. 'You could say he was under extreme provocation. You could say he was acting in self-defence. But they shot the dog afterwards. They had to shoot the dog.'

My father covered his eyes with his hands; and my mother cried: 'But, Denis, the tallboy is just a piece of furniture; and your father ...'

Denis said: 'My father's not here; but I think he would agree about what should be done with the tallboy. Although it would have broken his heart.'

Early next morning, before most people were about, Denis built a bonfire in the Hurrels' back garden. When it was going well, he fetched the tallboy: first the drawers, one by one; then the upper casing; then the lower, with its mutilated legs.

Watching from our back window, I saw the remains of the tallboy, as Denis carried them. You could see that it had once been big and beautiful – a pedigree thing, as Denis had said. But it wasn't just that the legs had been hacked and broken: everywhere the surface of the wood had been bruised and broken, the veneer splintered off. Regularly Wendy must have kicked at it and battered it, with whatever object came to her hand as a weapon. Those were the bangings I had heard, between her cursings, through the party-wall.

Denis put all the pieces on to the blazing bonfire, and they caught fire quickly and burnt, and burnt utterly away. By the next day the bonfire was nothing but a heap of white wood-ash, and Denis Hurrel had gone back to Scotland with his old mother.

And that evening, at dusk, when nobody was noticing, I climbed our fence and went to the bonfire. I sifted through the wood-ash with my fingers; and, in the end, I found three of those little brass stars that had winked at me from the centre of the tallboy's wooden drawer-knobs. They were blackened from the fire, but I pocketed them up; and later I cleaned them and polished them, till they shone like gold; and I have them still.

That's really the end of the story, I suppose. New people moved into the Hurrels' house next door, and I could hear them sometimes through the party-wall. But, when everything had gone quiet next door – in the middle of the night, for instance – I used to think I could hear something else: the ghost of a voice, or perhaps the voice of a ghost. Not the voice of old Mr Hurrel, returned to this world to lament the death of his beloved tallboy; not the voice of Wendy, murderous-sounding with jealousy and hatred; but another voice that was hardly a voice at all – an undertone that implored mercy, that pleaded for its life ...

I heard that voice, or thought I heard it, for as long as we lived in that house. I wonder if anyone, later, ever heard it. Or whether, anyway, with the passage of time, the voice failed and fell into silence, as do the voices of all things to which life has been given, or even lent.

The Hirn

This was a new motorway, and Mr Edward Edwards liked that. He liked new things – things newly designed and newly made. He drove his powerful car powerfully, just at the speed limit, eating up the miles, as the saying is – eating up as an impatient boa-constrictor might swallow its unimportant prey.

The new motorway sliced through new countryside. (Old countryside, really, but new to motorway travellers, and that was what mattered.) Open it was, with huge fields, mostly arable. Mr Edwards approved of the evident productivity.

He drove well, looking ahead at the road, keeping an eye on the rear-view mirror, and at the same time sparing casual glances towards the landscape on the right and on the left.

Something snagged in Mr Edwards's mind, suddenly:

there was an unexpected and unwelcome catching of his attention, as though on some country walk a hanging bramble had caught on his sleeve, on his arm. (But he had not gone on any country walk for many years.)

He glanced sharply to his left again.

To his left the gentle rise and fall of farmland was perhaps familiar ...

And that house ...

That farmhouse ...

Instantly Mr Edward Edwards had looked away from the farmhouse; but he could not prevent himself from remembering. He was driving his car as fast and as well as before, but he remembered. They say that, in the moment of drowning, a man may remember the whole of his past life, *see* it. In the moment of driving past Mortlock's, Mr Edward Edwards remembered everything, saw everything in his mind's eye, from long ago.

The farmhouse and farmlands had belonged to the Mortlocks for several generations; but in the last generation there had been no children. The heir was young Edward Edwards, from London, whose grandmother happened to have been a Mortlock.

After the funeral of his last elderly cousin, young Edward stayed on at Mortlock's to see exactly what his inheritance consisted of – and what further might be made of it. He knew nothing of farming, but already he knew about money and its uses. Already he knew what was what.

Above all, he was clever enough to know his own ignorance. He certainly did not intend – at least, at first – to try farming on his own. He might, however, put in an experienced farm manager – but keep an eye on him, too.

He suspected that a good deal could be done to improve on Mortlock methods of farming. He understood, for instance, that up-to-date farmers were grubbing up hedges to make larger, more economic fields. That was an obvious increase in efficiency. No land should be wasted; every acre – only he thought modernly in hectares – ought to be utilized. Total efficiency would be his aim – or rather, the aim of his farm manager.

Meanwhile, he had just a farm foreman: old Bill Hayes.

Bill Hayes was old only in the dialect of the countryside; in actuality, he was young middle-aged. That local inaccuracy of speech annoyed Edward Edwards. And, anyway, although Bill Hayes was not old in age, young Edward suspected him of being old in ideas.

In the company of his farm foreman, young Edward tramped purposefully over his fields, trying to understand what he saw, and to assess its value. Often, of course, he was baffled; then Bill Hayes would do his best to explain. Sometimes young Edward was satisfied. Sometimes, however, he made a suggestion or a criticism, which Bill Hayes would invariably show to be impractical, even foolish.

Edward Edwards began to dislike old Bill Hayes.

The only time he was certain of his opinion against the foreman's was over the Hirn. This was an area of trees, using up about a third of a hectare of land, in the middle of one of the best fields.

'What is it?' asked young Edward Edwards, staring across the stubbled earth to that secretive-looking clump of trees.

And old Bill had answered: 'It's Hirn.'

'Just some trees?'

'Well, there's water too, in the middle,' said old Bill. 'You could call it a pond.'

'But what's the point of it?'

And old Bill Hayes had repeated: 'It's Hirn.'

Somehow his careless omission, twice, of the 'the' that so obviously should have been there, irritated young

98

Edward. Again, there was that stupid suggestion of dialect, old worldness, and the rest. 'Well,' he said, 'the Hirn will have to justify its existence, if it's to remain. Otherwise, it goes.'

'Goes?'

'The land must be reclaimed for better use.'

'Better use? For Hirn?'

Young Edward thought: the fellow has an echo-chamber where his brains should be! Aloud, he said: 'If we get rid of the trees, and fill in this pond-place, then we can cultivate the land with the rest of the field.'

'I shouldn't do that, sir.'

'Why not?'

Old Bill Hayes did not answer.

'What's so special about the Hirn, then?'

Bill Hayes said: 'Well, after all, it is Hirn . . .'

Young Edward could get no further than that. But at least this senseless conversation made plain to him that he must get rid of old Bill Hayes as soon as possible. He needed a thoroughly rational, modern-minded farm manager: that was certain. This business of the Hirn was typical of what must have been going on, unchecked, during the Mortlock years.

Young Edward was pretty certain that the Hirn must be dealt with – and the sooner the better, of course. But he was not impulsive, not foolhardy. He would examine the site carefully for himself – and by himself – before coming to a decision. After all, there might even be valuable timber among those trees. (He was pleased with himself for the thought: surely, he was already learning.)

So the next day he set off alone in his car – not at all a car of the make, age, or condition that, in later years, he would care to have been seen driving. He knew the nearest point of access to the Hirn: a side road, along which had been built a line of Council houses. Just beyond the last house, on the same side, was a field-gate, and by this he parked. Through the gate, in the distance, he could already see the Hirn.

He climbed the gate and set off across the fields, passing by the side of the back garden of the last Council house. A woman was pegging out her washing, and a toddler played about beside the washing-basket. The toddler stopped playing to stare; but his mother went on with her work. Yet young Edward felt sure that she, too, was watching him. No wonder, perhaps – this little colony of houses was remote from most comings and goings.

A little later, as he was crossing the furrows, he looked back, to mark the gateway where he had left the car, and to see whether – yes, the two in the garden were now both openly staring after him. The woman held the child in her arms; and an old man had also come out of the house next door. He stood just the other side of the hedge from the woman and child, staring in the same direction.

Edward Edwards reached the Hirn. Even he could see that the woodland had been disgracefully neglected: no one had laid a finger on it for many, many years – perhaps ever, it seemed. The trees grew all anyhow: some strangled by ivy; some age-decayed and falling; some crippled by the fall of others; some young, but stunted and deformed in the struggle upwards to the sunlight. The space between the trees was dense with undergrowth.

It was very still, but no doubt there would be birds and other wild creatures. Young Edward peered about him. He could see no movement at all; but he supposed that beady bird-eyes would be watching him.

He began to push his way through the undergrowth between the trees, to find the water of which Bill Hayes had spoken.

He came to a small clearing – so it seemed – among the

trees: open, green, and almost eerily even. Absolutely flat. He hesitated at the edge of the clearing, and then, with a shock, realized that this was the water. Mantled by some over-spreading tiny plant life, it had seemed to him to be solid, turfy land. He had almost fallen into the pond – almost walked into it.

There was no knowing how deep the water was.

The water was unmoving, except perhaps at its edges, where he thought he saw, out of the corner of his eye, a slight stirring. Perhaps tadpoles? But was this the season for tadpoles? He tried to remember; but he had never been much of a tadpole boy, even with the few opportunities that London offered. He had always hated that dark wriggliness.

He decided to complete his examination by walking round the edge of the pond. This turned out to be difficult, because of the thickly growing vegetation. At one place a bush leant in a straggly way over the water; it bore clusters of tiny, dark-purple berries. He thought that these must be elderberries, and he knew you could eat elderberries. He stretched out a hand to pick some, and then thought that perhaps these were not elderberries; perhaps another kind of fruit; perhaps poisonous. He drew his hand back sharply. He felt endangered.

And then he saw the amazing oak. The trunk must have been at least two metres across at its base, but the tree was quite hollow, with some other younger tree boldly growing up in the middle of it. All the same, the oak was not dead: from its crust of bark twigs and leaves had spurted. And at some time someone – apparently to keep this shell of a tree from falling apart – had put a steel cable round it.

'Pointless,' said young Edward to himself. Because of the elderberries – if they had been elderberries – he had felt afraid, and that still angered him. Now the sight of the giant oak, whose collapse was thus futilely delayed, angered him even more.

He pushed his way out of the little piece of woodland to its far side and the open field beyond. From there the Council houses were not visible. The Hirn lay between.

The shortest way back to the field-gate and his car would have been by the path his pushing and trampling had already made through the woodland. But he decided not to re-enter the Hirn. He preferred to take the long way round the outside, until he was in view of the houses, the gate, the car.

When he could see the Council houses, he could see that the woman and child were still in their garden; also the old man in his. When they saw him coming, they went indoors.

'I don't know what they thought they were going to see,' young Edward said to himself resentfully. 'Something – oh, *very* extraordinary, no doubt!'

He went straight back to the car, and then home. His examination of the Hirn had been quick but thorough enough. There had been nothing much to see; and, frankly, he did not like the place.

The next day he tackled old Bill Hayes and told him that the Hirn must be obliterated. He did not use the word, but it was in his mind as he gave the order. After all, he was owner and master.

Old Bill Hayes looked at him: 'But it's Hirn,' he said.

'So you mentioned before,' said young Edward, knowing that this sarcasm would be wasted on Bill's dullness. 'All the same, see that what I want is done.'

Old Bill Hayes made no further objection; but neither did he do anything in the days that followed.

Then, realizing that his wishes had been ignored, Edward gave the order again.

Again, nothing happened.

This time, his blood up, young Edward acted for himself, without consulting or even informing old Bill Hayes. He made the right inquiries and was able to arrange for an outside firm to do the clearance job. They said it would take several days. They would start by cutting down all the trees. The timber – valueless, of course – and the brushwood would then be cleared. Remaining tree-stumps and roots must all be grubbed up; otherwise they would grow again, even more strongly. Finally, the pond would be filled in and the whole site levelled.

In only a short time, all trace of the Hirn would have disappeared.

On the first day of the operation, young Edward Edwards had a morning appointment with the manager of the local bank where the Mortlocks had always done business. There were financial matters still to be sorted out. But, on top of these, the manager annoyed young Edward with unwanted advice. He strongly urged him not to take on the Mortlock farm on his own account, even with a farm manager. It would be more sensible (the bank manager said) to sell the farm and farmhouse, and use the money in some business which he was more likely fully to understand.

Young Edward was furious.

His fury lasted into the afternoon, when he decided that he was in just the mood to inspect the destruction of the Hirn. Besides, he somehow felt that he ought to be there – perhaps as a witness to the execution.

He drove his car to the same place as before, and set off again across the fields. It was easy to see where the gang had been before him, with their heavily loaded vehicles, and he could already see where they had been at work: the treed area of the Hirn was now only about a tenth of its original size. The other nine-tenths had been roughly cleared, leaving freshly cut tree-stumps sticking up everywhere like jagged teeth.

The gang themselves had gone home. He was disappointed – and disapproving – that they had chosen to stop work so early.

Once, before he reached what was left of the Hirn, young Edward looked back over the fields to the Council houses. No one at all in the gardens. No lights yet in any windows, as there would be soon; but he was aware of something – a pallor behind a window-glass: a face looking out in his direction. From more than one window he fancied that they watched him.

He was soon picking his way among the many tree-stumps, making for the few trees that were left standing near the pond. The dying oak had been left standing. It survived. He stared at it. Unwillingly he came to the decision that he wanted to touch it. He went right up to it and laid the flat of his hand against the bark. For the first time it occurred to him to wonder how old the tree might be. People said that oaks could live for hundreds of years ... hundreds and hundreds of years ...

He decided that he had seen enough of the Hirn. He turned away from the oak, to get out of this tiny remnant of woodland. Tiny it might be, but it was thick – thicker than he had noticed on his coming. He had to push his way through the undergrowth – perhaps because this was not the way he had come, but a new way. Certainly it had been much easier for him to reach the oak than, now, it was for him to get away from it.

The end of the afternoon was coming; the light was failing.

He came to the pond. The water looked almost black now. To his surprise he saw that there were still trees and bushes crowding the banks round it: he had thought, as he came over the fields, that they had been cut down.

He turned away from the water in the direction – he thought – of the Council houses and his parked car. He must have made a mistake, however, for he re-entered untouched woodland again.

He was angered at how long it was taking him to get out of this wretched grove of trees.

He came to the oak again, and turned from it abruptly to struggle on through the undergrowth in the direction he supposed to be the right one. The only sound was the sound of his crashing about and his own heavy breathing; and then he thought – or perhaps he imagined? – he was hearing something else. He stopped to listen carefully . . .

(Driving fast along the motorway, Mr Edwards remembered standing still to listen so carefully, so very carefully. As he drove, his hands tightened on the driving-wheel until his knuckles whitened . . .)

Young Edward Edwards listened . . .

It was very quiet. Everywhere round him was now still and very, very quiet. But, all the same, he thought there was something – not a sound that began and ended, but a sound that was there, as the wood was there. The sound enclosed him, as the wood enclosed him.

The sound was of someone trying not to laugh – of someone privately amused – quietly and maliciously amused.

Young Edward made a rush forward, and reached the pond again.

He stood there, and the sound was there with him, all around him. He stared at the blackness of the water until he could feel his eyes beginning to trick him. He watched the water, and the water seemed to watch him. The surface of the blackness seemed to shiver, to shudder; the edges of the water seemed to crinkle. The mantle of black on the surface of the water seemed to be gathering itself up, as a woman's garments are gathered, before the woman herself rises . . .

(Along the motorway Mr Edwards drove fast, trying to think of nothing but the motorway; but he had to remember . . .)

Young Edward ran; he was trying to run; he was trying to escape. The sound was still round him; and round him now, everywhere, trees stood in his way and the undergrowth spread wide to catch him. They all baited him, for someone's private amusement. He fought to run: a bramble snagged in his sleeve, and then tried to drag the coat from his back; an elder branch whipped him across the face; a sly tree-root tripped him.

He tripped. He was falling.

He knew that he was falling among tall trees and thickets of undergrowth; and that he was lost – forever lost! He gave a long scream, but a blow on the head finished the scream, and also finished young Edward Edwards for the time being.

In the Council houses they heard the long scream that suddenly stopped, and a little party set off hurriedly to find young Mr Edwards. They had been waiting for something to happen. They were not callous people, only very fearful; otherwise they might have gone earlier.

They found him lying among the tree-stumps of the cleared part of the woodland. He had fallen head-first on to one of them. Later, in hospital, he was told that he had been very lucky: he might so easily have split his whole head open on that jagged tree-stump. Killed himself.

And later still, in London (where he had insisted on going, straight from the hospital), he had instructed the bank to arrange for the immediate sale of Mortlock's, farmhouse and farm, the lot. That had been done, most profitably, and he had never seen the place again – until today, from the motorway.

As he drove, he ventured another quick glance to his left: the farmhouse was no longer in sight. His spirits lifted. These must still be Mortlock fields, but they would soon be passed, too.

Then he saw the Council houses, and recognized them . . .

Then the big field . . .

Then, in the middle, green and flourishing, a coppice of trees . . .

He had been warned that, unless they were grubbed up by the roots, the tree-stumps would sprout and grow even more strongly. Yes, they had grown; and now, as once before, thick woodland hid from sight that mantled water. And he began to think he heard – borne on some unlikely wind – the faintest sound of unkind laughter.

Mr Edwards brought his gaze back strictly to the motorway ahead, turned the car radio on to full volume, accelerated well over the speed limit, and so passed beyond further sight of the trees that were Hirn.

He put view and sound, and remembrance of both, behind him for good. He had made up his mind, for good: he would not drive this way again. There were always other roads, and other modes of travel – rail, air. He would never use this motorway again.

He never did.

The Yellow Ball

The ladder reached comfortably to the branch of the sycamore they had decided on; and its foot was held steady by Lizzie, while her father climbed up. He carried the rope – nylon, for strength – in loops over his shoulder. He knotted one end securely round the chosen branch, and then let the other end drop. It fell to dangle only a little to one side of where Con held the old car-tyre upright on the ground. Really, of course, there was no need for the tyre to be held in that position yet; but something had to be found for Con to do, to take his mind off the cows in the meadow. He was nervous of animals, and cows were large.

Their father prepared to descend the ladder.

And then – how exactly did it happen? Why did it happen? Was Con really the first to notice the knot-hole in the tree-trunk, as he later claimed? Or did Lizzie point it out? Would their father, anyway, have reached over sideways from the ladder – as he now did – to dip his fingers into the cavity?

'There's something in here ... something stuck ...' He teetered a little on the ladder as he tugged. 'Got it!'

And, as he grasped whatever was in the hole, the air round the group in the meadow tightened, tautened with expectancy –

Something was going to happen ...

Going to happen ...

To happen ...

'Here we are!' He was holding aloft a dingy, spherical object. 'A ball – it's a ball! A chance in a thousand: someone threw a ball high, and it happened to lodge here! No, a chance in a million for it to have happened like that!'

He dropped the ball. Lizzie tried to catch it, but was prevented by the ladder. Con tried, but was prevented by the tyre he held. The ball bounced, but not high, rolled out a little way over the meadow, came to rest.

And something invisibly in the meadow breathed again, watchful, but relaxed ...

The two children forgot the ball, because their father was now down from the ladder: he was knotting the free end of the rope round the tyre, so that it cleared the ground by about half a metre. It hung there, enticingly.

While their father put his ladder away, the children began arguing about who should have first go on the tyre. He came back, sharply stopped their quarrelling, and showed them how both could get on at the same time: they must face each other, with both pairs of legs through the circle of the tyre, but in opposite directions. So they sat on the lowest curve of the tyre, gripping the rope from which it hung; and their father began to swing them, higher and higher, wider and wider.

As they swung up, the setting sun was in their eyes, and suddenly they saw the whole of the meadow, but tilted, tipped; and they saw the houses on the other side of the meadow rushing towards them; and then as they swung back again, the houses were rushing away, and the meadow too –

Swinging – swinging – they whooped and shrieked for joy.

Their mother came out to watch for a little, and then said they must all come in for tea. So all three went in, through the little gate from the meadow into the garden, and then into the house. They left the tyre still swaying; they left the dirty old ball where it had rolled and come to rest and been forgotten.

As soon as he had finished his tea, Con was eager to be in the meadow, to have the tyre to himself while there was still daylight. Lizzie went on munching.

But, in a few moments, he was indoors again, saying hesitantly: 'I think – I think there's someone in the meadow waiting for me.'

Their father said: 'Nonsense, boy! The cows will never hurt you!'

'It's not the cows at all. There's someone waiting. For me.'

Their mother looked at their father: 'Perhaps . . .'

'I'll come out with you,' he said to Con; and so he did; and Lizzie followed them both.

But Con was saying: 'I didn't say I was afraid. I just said there was someone in the meadow. I thought there was. That's all.' They went through the garden gate into the meadow. 'Man or woman?' Con's father asked him. 'Or boy or girl?'

'No,' said Con. 'It wasn't like that.'

His father had scanned the wide meadow thoroughly. 'No one at all.' He sighed. 'Oh, Conrad, your *imagina-*

tion! I'm going back before the tea's too cold. You two can stay a bit longer, if you like. Till it begins to get dark.'

He went indoors.

Lizzie, looking beyond the tyre, and remembering after all, said: 'That ball's gone.'

'I picked it up.' Con brought it out of his pocket, held it out to Lizzie. She took it. It was smaller than a tennis-ball, but heavier, because solid. One could see that it was yellow under the dirtiness – and it was not really so very dirty after all. Dirt had collected in the tiny, shallow holes with which the surface of the ball was pitted. That was all.

'I wonder what made the holes,' said Lizzie.

Con held out his hand for the ball again. Lizzie did not give up: 'It's just as much mine as yours.' They glared at each other, but uneasily. They did not really *want* to quarrel about this ball; this ball was for better things than that.

'I suppose we could take turns at having it,' said Lizzie. 'Or perhaps you don't really want the ball, Con?'

'But I do – I do!' At the second 'do' he lunged forward, snatched the ball from his sister and was through the gate with it, back towards the house – and Lizzie was after him. The gate clicked shut behind them both –

Suddenly they both stopped, and turned to look back. Oh! they knew that something was coming –

High, and over –

They saw it – or rather, they *had* seen it, for it happened so swiftly –

A small, dark shape, a shadow had leapt the shut gate after them – elegant as a dancer in flying motion – eager –

Con breathed: 'Did you see him?'

'Her,' Lizzie whispered back. 'A bitch. I saw the teats, as she came over the gate.'

'Her ears lifted in the wind ...'

'She had her eyes on the ball – oh, Con! It's *her* ball! Hers! She wants it – she wants it!'

Though nothing was visible now, they could feel the air of the garden quivering with hope and expectancy.

'Throw it for her, Con!' Lizzie urged him. 'Throw it!'

With all his strength, Con threw the yellow ball over the gate and out into the meadow, and the shadow of a shape followed it in another noble leap and then a long darting movement across the meadow, straight as an arrow after the ball, seeming to gain on it, to be about to catch up with it, to catch it –

But when the ball came to rest, the other movement still went on, not in a straight line any more, but sweeping to and fro, quartering the ground, seeking – seeking –

'It's her ball: why doesn't she find it and pick it up?' Con asked wonderingly. 'It's there for her.'

Lizzie said: 'I think – I think it's because it's a real ball, and she's not a real dog. She can't pick it up, poor thing; she's only some kind of ghost.'

A ghost! Con said nothing, but drew closer to his sister. They stood together in the garden, looking out into the meadow, while they accustomed their minds to what they were seeing. They stood on the solid earth of the garden-path; behind them was their house, with the lights now on and their father drinking his cups of tea; in front of them lay the meadow with the sycamore tree; in the far distance, the cows.

All real, all solid, all familiar.

And in the middle of the meadow – to and fro, to and fro – moved the ghost of a dog.

But now Con moved away from his sister, stood stalwartly alone again. An ordinary ghost might have frightened him for longer; a real dog would certainly have frightened him. But the ghost of a dog – that was different!

'Lizzie,' he said, 'let's not tell anyone. Not anyone. It's our private ghost. Just ours.'

'All right.'

They continued gazing over the meadow until they could see no longer through the deepening dusk. Then their mother was rapping on the window for them to come indoors, and they had to go.

Indoors, their parents asked them: 'Did you have a good swing on the tyre?'

'The tyre?' They stared, and said: 'We forgot.'

Later, they went into the meadow again with a torch to look for the yellow ball. They were on the alert, but there was now nobody, nothing that was waiting – even when Con, holding the ball in his hand, pretended that he was about to throw it. No ardent expectation. Nothing now but the meadow and the trees in it and the unsurprised cows.

They brought the ball indoors and scrubbed it as clean as they could with a nailbrush; but there would always be dirt in the little holes. 'Those are toothmarks,' said Con.

'Hers,' said Lizzie. 'This was her own special ball that she used to carry in her mouth when she was alive, when she was a flesh-and-blood dog.'

'Where did she live?' asked Con. But, of course, Lizzie didn't know: perhaps in one of the houses by the meadow; perhaps even in their own, before ever they came to it.

'Shall we see her tomorrow?' asked Con. 'Oh, I want to see her again tomorrow!'

The next day they took the yellow ball into the meadow before school, but with no result. They tried again as soon as they got home: nothing. They had their tea and went out to the tyre again with the yellow ball. Nobody – nothing – was waiting for them. So they settled themselves on the tyre and swung to and fro, but gently, and talking to each other in low voices; and the sun began to set.

It was almost dusk, and they were still gently swinging, when Lizzie whispered: 'She's here now – I'm sure of it!' Lizzie had been holding on to the nylon rope with one hand only, because the other held the yellow ball – it was her turn with it today, they had decided. Now she put her feet down to stop the swinging of the tyre, and stepped out from it altogether.

'Here, you!' she called softly; and, aside to Con, 'Oh, I wish we knew her name!'

'Don't bother about that,' said Con. 'Throw the ball!'

So Lizzie did. They both saw where it went; also they glimpsed the flashing speed that followed it. And then began the fruitless searching, to and fro, to and fro . . .

'The poor thing!' said Lizzie, watching.

Con was only pleased and excited. He still sat on the tyre, and now he began to push hard with his toes, to swing higher and higher, chanting under his breath: 'We've got a ghost – a ghooooost! We've got a ghost – a ghooooost!' Twice he stopped his swinging and chanting and left the tyre to fetch the ball and throw it again. (Lizzie did not want to throw it.) Each time they watched the straight following of the ball and then the spreading search that could not possibly have an end. But when darkness began to fall, they felt suddenly that there was no more ghost in the meadow; and it was time for them to go indoors, too.

As they went, Con said, almost shyly: 'Tomorrow, when it's really my turn, do you think if I held the ball out to her and sort of *tempted* her with it, that she'd come close up to me? I might touch her . . .'

Lizzie said: 'You can't touch a ghost. And besides, Con, you're frightened of dogs. You know you are. Else we might have had one of our own – a real one – years ago.'

Con simply said: 'This dog is different. I like this dog.'

This first evening with the ghost-dog was only a beginning. Every day now they took the yellow ball into the meadow. They soon found that their ghost-dog came only at sunset, at dusk. Someone in the past had made a habit of giving this dog a ball-game in the evening, before going indoors for the night. A ball-game – that was all the dog hoped for. That was why she came at the end of the day, whenever a human hand held the yellow ball.

'And I think I can guess why Dad found the ball where he did, high up a tree,' said Lizzie. 'It was put there deliberately, after the dog had died. Someone – probably the person who owned the dog – put it where no one was ever likely to find it. That someone wanted the ball not to be thrown again, because it was a haunted ball, you might say. It would draw the dog – the ghost of the dog – to come back to chase it and search for it and never find it. Never find it. Never.'

'You make everything sound sad and wrong,' said Con. 'But it isn't, really.'

Lizzie did not answer.

They had settled into a routine with their ghost-dog. They kept her yellow ball inside the hollow of the tyre, and brought it out every evening to throw it, in turns. Con always threw in his turn, but Lizzie often did not want to for hers. Then Con wanted to have her turn for himself, and at first she let him. Then she changed her mind: she insisted that, on her evenings, neither of them threw. Con was annoyed ('Dog-in-the-manger,' he muttered), but, after all, Lizzie had the right.

A Saturday was coming when neither of them would throw, for a different reason. There was going to be a family expedition to the Zoo, in London; they were all going on a cheap day-excursion by train; and they would not be home until well after dark.

The day came, and the visit to the Zoo went as well as such visits do; and now at last they were on the train again, going home. All four were tired, but only their parents were dozing. Con was wide awake, and excited by the train. He pointed out to Lizzie that all the lights had come on inside the railway carriage; outside, the view was of dark landscapes and the sparkling illumination of towns, villages and highways.

The ticket-inspector came round, and Lizzie nudged their father awake. He found their four tickets, and they were clipped.

'And what about the dog?' said the ticket-inspector with severity.

'Dog?' Their father was still half-asleep, confused.

'Your dog. It should have a ticket. And why isn't it in the guard's van?'

'But there's no dog! We haven't a dog with us. We don't own a dog.'

'I saw one,' said the inspector grimly. He stooped and began looking under the seats; and other passengers began looking too, even while they all agreed that they had seen no dog.

And there really was no dog.

'Sorry, sir,' said the ticket-inspector at last. His odd mistake had shaken him. 'I could have sworn I saw something move that was a dog.' He took off his glasses and worried at the lenses with his handkerchief, and passed on.

The passengers resettled themselves; and when their own parents were dozing off again, Lizzie whispered to Con: 'Con, you little demon! You brought it with you – the yellow ball!'

'Yes!' He held his pocket a little open and towards her, so that she saw the ball nestling inside. 'And I had my hand on it, holding it, when the ticket-man came to us. And it worked! It worked!' He was so pleased with himself that he was bouncing up and down in his seat.

Lizzie said in a furious whisper: 'You should never have done it! Think how terrified that dog must have been to find herself on a train – a *train*! Con, how could you treat a dog so?'

'She was all right,' Con said stubbornly. 'She can't come to any harm, anyway: she's not a dog, she's only the ghost of one. And, anyway, it's as much my yellow ball as yours. We each have a half share in it.'

'You never asked my permission about my half of the ball,' said Lizzie, 'and don't talk so loud, someone will hear.'

They talked no more in so public a place; nor when they got home. They all went straight to bed, and all slept late the next morning, Sunday.

All except for Lizzie; she was up early, for her own purposes. She crept into Con's room, as he slept, and took the yellow ball from his pocket. She took it down the garden path to her father's work-shed, at the bottom. She and the yellow ball went inside, and Lizzie shut the door behind them.

Much later, when he was swinging on the tyre in the morning sunshine, Con saw Lizzie coming into the meadow. He called to her: 'All right! I know you've taken it, so there! You can have it today, anyway; but it's my turn tomorrow. We share the yellow ball. Remember?'

Lizzie came close to him. She held out towards him her right hand, closed; then she opened it carefully, palm upwards. 'Yours,' she said. On her flattened palm sat the domed shape of half the yellow ball. She twisted her hand slightly, so that the yellow dome fell on its side: then Con could see the sawn cross-section – black except for the outer rim of yellow.

For a moment Con was stunned. Then he screamed at her: 'Wherever you hide your half, I'll find it! I'll glue the halves together! I'll make the yellow ball again and I'll throw it – I'll throw it and I'll throw it and I'll throw it!'

'No, you won't,' said Lizzie. This time she held out towards him her cupped left hand: he saw a mess of chips and crumbs and granules of black, dotted with yellow. It had taken Lizzie a long time in her father's workshop to saw and cut and chip and grate her half-ball down to this. She said flatly: 'I've destroyed the yellow ball for ever.' Then, with a gesture of horror, she flung the ball-particles from her and burst into a storm of sobbing and crying.

Only the shock of seeing Lizzie crying in such a way – she rarely cried at all – stopped Con from going for her with fists and feet and teeth as well. But the grief and desolation that he saw in Lizzie made him know his own affliction: grief at loss overwhelmed his first rage, and he began to cry, too.

'Why did you have to do that to the yellow ball, Lizzie? Why didn't you just hide it from me? Up a tree again: I might not have found it.'

'Somebody would have found it, some day . . .'

'Or in the earth: you could have dug a deep hole, Lizzie.'

'Somebody would have found it . . .'

'Oh, it wasn't fair of you, Lizzie!'

'No, it wasn't fair. But it was the only way. Otherwise she would search for ever for something she could never find.'

'Go away,' said Con.

Lizzie picked up the half-ball from the ground, where she had let it fall. She took it back with her to the house, to the dustbin. Then she went indoors and upstairs to her bedroom and lay down on her bed and cried again.

They kept apart all day, as far as possible; but, in the early evening, Lizzie saw Con on the tyre, and she went out to him, and he let her swing him gently to and fro. After a while he said: 'We'll never see her again, shall we?'

'No,' said Lizzie; 'but at least she won't be worried and disappointed and unhappy again, either.'

'I just miss her so,' said Con. 'If we can't have the ghost of a dog, I wish we had a real dog.'

'But, Con –'

'No, truly, I wouldn't be frightened if we had a dog like her – just like her. It would have to be a bitch – she was black, wasn't she, Lizzie?'

'I thought so. A glossy black. I remember, her collar was red. Red against black: it looked smart.'

'A glossy black bitch with a whippy tail and those big soft ears that flew out. That's what I'd like.'

'Oh, Con!' cried Lizzie. She had always longed for them to have a dog; and it had never been possible because of Con's terrors. Until now . . .

Con was still working things out: 'And she must be a jumper and a runner and she must *love* running after a ball. And we'll call her – what ought we to call her, Lizzie?'

'I don't know . . .'

'It must be exactly the right name – *exactly* right . . .'

He had stopped swinging; Lizzie had stopped pushing him. They remained quite still under the sycamore tree, thinking.

Then they began to feel it: something was going to happen . . .

For one last time; a quittance for them . . .

The sun had already set; daylight was fading. 'What is it – what's happening?' whispered Con, preparing to step out of the tyre, afraid.

'Wait, Con. I think I know.' Thinking, foreseeing, Lizzie knew. 'The ball's destroyed; it's a ghost-ball now; a ghost-ball for a ghost-dog. Look, Con! It's being thrown!'

'*Being thrown?*' repeated Con. 'But – but – *who's* throwing it?'

'I don't know; but look – oh, look, Con!'

They could not see the thrower at all, but they thought they could see the ghost of a ball; and they could certainly see the dog. She waited for the throw, and then – on the instant – was after the ball in a straight line of speed, and caught up with it, and caught it, and was carried onwards with the force of her own velocity, but directed her course and began to come back in a wide, happy, unhurried curve. The yellow ball was between her teeth, and her tail was up in triumph – a thing they had never seen before. She brought the ball back to the thrower; and the thrower threw again, and again she ran, and caught, and came loping back. Again; and again; and again.

They could not see the thrower at all, but once the ghost of a voice – and still they could not tell: man, woman, boy, or girl? – called to the dog.

'Listen!' whispered Lizzie; but they did not hear the voice again.

They watched until darkness fell and the throwing ceased.

Con said: 'What was her name? Nellie? Jilly?'

Lizzie said: 'No, Millie.'

'Millie?'

'It's short for Millicent, I think. An old name: Millicent.'

'I'm glad now about the yellow ball,' said Con. 'And we'll call her Millicent – Millie for short.'

'Her?'

'You know: our dog.'

They left the tyre under the sycamore and went indoors to tackle their parents.

THE PRIME MINISTER'S BRAIN   *Gillian Cross*

The fiendish Demon Headmaster plans to gain control of No. 10 Downing Street and lure the Prime Minister into his evil clutches.

JASON BODGER AND THE PRIORY GHOST
Gene Kemp

A ghost story, both funny and exciting, about Jason, the bane of every teacher's life, who is pursued by the ghost of a little nun from the twelfth century!

HALFWAY ACROSS THE GALAXY AND TURN LEFT
Robin Klein

A humorous account of what happens to a family banished from their planet, Zygron, when they have to spend a period of exile on Earth.

SUPER GRAN TO THE RESCUE   *Forrest Wilson*

The punchpacking, baddiebiffing escapades of the world's No. 1 senior citizen superhero – Super Gran! Now a devastating series on ITV!

TOM TIDDLER'S GROUND   *John Rowe Townsend*

Vic and Brain are given an old rowing boat which leads to the unravelling of a mystery and a happy reunion of two friends. An exciting adventure story.

JELLYBEAN *Tessa Duder*

A sensitive modern novel about Geraldine, alias 'Jellybean', who leads a rather solitary life as the only child of a single parent. She's tired of having to fit in with her mother's busy schedule, but a new friend and a performance of *The Nutcracker Suite* change everything.

THE PRIESTS OF FERRIS *Maurice Gee*

Susan Ferris and her cousin Nick return to the world of O, which they had saved from the evil Halfmen, only to find that O is now ruled by cruel and ruthless priests. Can they save the inhabitants of O from tyranny? An action-packed and gripping story by the author of the prize-winning *The Halfmen of O*.

THE SEA IS SINGING *Rosalind Kerven*

In her seaside Shetland home, Tess is torn between the plight of the whales and loyalty to her father and his job on the oil rig. A haunting and thought-provoking novel.

BACK HOME *Michelle Magorian*

A marvellously gripping story of an irrepressible girl's struggle to adjust to a new life. Twelve-year-old Rusty, who had been evacuated to the United States when she was seven, returns to the grey austerity of post-war Britain.